By C. S. Forester

The Hornblower Saga

MR. MIDSHIPMAN HORNBLOWER

LIEUTENANT HORNBLOWER

HORNBLOWER AND THE HOTSPUR

HORNBLOWER DURING THE CRISIS

HORNBLOWER AND THE ATROPOS

BEAT TO QUARTERS

SHIP OF THE LINE

FLYING COLOURS

COMMODORE HORNBLOWER

LORD HORNBLOWER

ADMIRAL HORNBLOWER IN THE WEST INDIES

YOUNG HORNBLOWER

(*A reprint including* Mr. Midshipman Hornblower, Lieutenant Hornblower, *and* Hornblower and the *Atropos*)

CAPTAIN HORATIO HORNBLOWER

(*A reprint including* Beat to Quarters, Ship of the Line, *and* Flying Colours)

THE INDOMITABLE HORNBLOWER

(*A reprint including* Commodore Hornblower, Lord Hornblower, *and* Admiral Hornblower in the West Indies)

THE HORNBLOWER COMPANION

Also

THE GUN · THE PEACEMAKER · THE AFRICAN QUEEN ·

THE GENERAL

TO THE INDIES · THE CAPTAIN FROM CONNECTICUT ·

PAYMENT DEFERRED

RIFLEMAN DODD AND THE GUN: TWO NOVELS OF THE

PENINSULAR CAMPAIGNS

(Rifleman Dodd *was published in England under the title* Death to the French)

THE SHIP · THE SKY AND THE FOREST

RANDALL AND THE RIVER OF TIME · THE NIGHTMARE ·

THE GOOD SHEPHERD

THE LAST NINE DAYS OF THE BISMARCK

Hornblower During the Crisis

HORNBLOWER
During the Crisis

and Two Stories
HORNBLOWER'S TEMPTATION
and
THE LAST ENCOUNTER

by C. S. FORESTER

Little, Brown and Company · Boston · Toronto

FIRST EDITION

*Published simultaneously in Canada
by Little, Brown & Company (Canada) Limited*

PRINTED IN THE UNITED STATES OF AMERICA

C. S. Forester's devoted readers were immeas-
urably saddened to learn of his death in April
1966. As usual, he was then in the process of
writing another novel dealing with the career of
the indomitable Horatio Hornblower. Although
he was not allowed to complete this story, from
the notes he left behind it is possible to see how
it would have ended. These notes follow Hornblower During the Crisis.

Contents

Hornblower During the Crisis

I

HORNBLOWER was expecting the knock on the door, because he had seen through his cabin window enough to guess what was happening outside.

"Water-hoy coming alongside, sir," reported Bush, hat in hand.

"Very well, Mr. Bush." Hornblower was disturbed in spirit and had no intention of smoothing Bush's path for him.

"The new captain's on board the hoy, sir." Bush was perfectly well aware of Hornblower's mood, yet was not ingenious enough to cope with it.

"Very well, Mr. Bush."

But that was simple cruelty, the deliberate teasing of a nearly dumb animal; Hornblower realised that such behaviour really gave him no pleasure and only occasioned embarrassment to Bush. He relented to the extent of introducing a lighter touch into the conversation.

"So now you have a few minutes to spare for me, Mr. Bush?" he said. "It's a change after your preoccupation of the last two days."

That was neither fair nor kind, and Bush showed his feelings in his face.

"I've had my duties to do, sir," he mumbled.

"Getting *Hotspur* into apple-pie order ready for her new captain?"

"Y-yes, sir."

"Doesn't matter about me, of course. I'm only a back number now."

"Sir—"

Even though he was not in a smiling mood, Hornblower could not help smiling at the misery of Bush's expression.

"I'm glad to see you're only human, Mr. Bush, after all. Sometimes I've doubted it. There couldn't be a more perfect first lieutenant."

Bush needed two or three seconds in which to digest this unexpected compliment.

"That's very good of you, sir. Very kind indeed. But it's been all your doing."

In a moment they would slide down the slippery slopes of sentiment, which would be unbearable.

"Time for me to appear on deck," said Hornblower. "We'd better say goodbye, Mr. Bush. The best of luck under your new captain."

He went so far towards yielding to the mood of the moment as to hold out his hand, which Bush took. Luckily Bush's emotions prevented him from saying more than just "Goodbye, sir," and Hornblower hurried out through the cabin door with Bush at his heels.

There was instantly plenty of distraction as the water-hoy was laid alongside the *Hotspur;* the side of the hoy was covered from end to end with old sails in rolls and with substantial fend-offs of sandbags, yet it was a ticklish business, even in the sheltered waters of this little bay, to pass lines between the two ships and draw them together. A gangplank came clattering out from the hoy to bridge the gap between the two decks, and a burly man in full uniform made the precarious crossing. He was very tall—two or three inches over six feet—and heavily built; a man of middle age or more, to judge by the shock of grey hair revealed when he raised his hat. The boatswain's mates pealed loudly on their calls; the two ship's drummers beat a ragged ruffle.

"Welcome aboard, sir," said Hornblower.

The new captain pulled a paper from his breast pocket, opened it, and began to read. A shout from Bush bared every head so that the function would take place with due solemnity.

"Orders given by us, William Cornwallis, Vice Admiral of the Red, Knight of the Most Honourable Order of the Bath, Commanding His Majesty's Ships and Vessels of the Channel Fleet, to James Percival Meadows, Esquire—"

"D'ye think we have all day?" This was a new, stentorian voice from the deck of the hoy. "Stand by to take the hoses, there! Mr. Lieutenant, let's have some hands for the pumps."

The voice came, appropriately enough, from the barrel-shaped captain of the hoy. Bush signalled frantically for him to stay quiet until this vital ceremonial was completed.

"Time enough for that tomfoolery when the water's

all aboard. The wind'll shift within the hour," roared the barrel-shaped captain, quite unabashed. Captain Meadows scowled and hesitated, but for all his vast stature he could do nothing to silence the captain of the hoy. He roared through the rest of his orders at a pace nearer a gallop than a canter, and folded them up with evident relief now that he was legally captain of H.M.S. *Hotspur*.

"On hats!" bellowed Bush.

"Sir, I relieve you," said Meadows to Hornblower.

"I much regret the bad manners displayed in the hoy, sir," said Hornblower to Meadows.

"Now let's have some sturdy hands," said the barrel-shaped captain to no one in particular, and Meadows shrugged his vast shoulders with resignation.

"Mr. Bush, my first lieutenant—I mean your first lieutenant, sir," said Hornblower, hastily effecting the introduction.

"Carry on, Mr. Bush," said Meadows, and Bush plunged instantly into the business of transferring the fresh water from the hoy.

"Who's that fellow, sir?" asked Hornblower, with a jerk of his thumb at the captain of the hoy.

"He's been my cross for the last two days," answered Meadows. "He's not only captain but he's thirty-seven sixty-fourths owner. Under Navy Office contract—can't press him, can't press his men, as they all have protections. Says what he likes, does what he likes, and I'd give my prize money for the next five years to have him at the gratings for ten minutes."

"M'm," said Hornblower. "I'm taking passage with him."

"Hope you fare better than I did."

"By your leave, sirs." A hand from the hoy came pushing along the gangplank dragging a canvas hose. At his heels came someone carrying papers; there was bustle everywhere.

"I'll hand over the ship's papers, sir," said Hornblower. "Will you come with me? I mean—they are ready in your cabin when you have time to attend to them, sir."

In the cabin, his sea-chest and ditty bag lay forlorn on the bare deck, pathetic indications of his immediate departure. It was the work only of a few moments to complete the transfer of command.

"May I request of Mr. Bush the loan of a hand to transfer my dunnage, sir?" asked Hornblower.

Now he was nobody. He was not even a passenger; he had no standing at all, and this became more evident still when he returned to the deck to look round for his officers to bid them farewell. They were all engrossed in the business of the moment, with hardly a second to spare for him. Handshakes were hasty and perfunctory; it was with a queer relief that he turned away to the gangplank.

It was a relief that was short-lived, for even at anchor *Hotspur* was rolling perceptibly in the swell that curved in round the point, and the two ships, *Hotspur* and the water-hoy, were rolling in opposite phases, their upper works inclining first together and then away from each

7

other, so that the gangplank which joined them was possessed of several distinct motions—it swung in a vertical plane like a seesaw and in a horizontal plane like a compass needle. It rose and fell bodily, too, but the most frightening motion, instantly obvious as soon as he addressed himself to the crossing, was a stabbing back-and-forth motion as the ships surged together and apart, the gap bridged by the plank being now six feet and then sixteen. To a barefooted seaman the passage would be nothing; to Hornblower it was a rather frightening matter—an eighteen-inch plank with no handrail. He was conscious, too, of the barrel-shaped captain watching him, but at least that made him determined to show no hesitation once he decided on the passage. He studied the motions of the plank out of the tail of his eye while apparently his attention was fully taken up by the various activities in the two ships.

Then he made a rush for it, got both feet on the plank, endured a nightmare interval when it seemed as if, hurry as he would, he made no progress at all, and then thankfully reached the end of the plank and stepped clear of it onto the comparative stability of the deck. The barrel-shaped captain made no move to welcome him, and while two hands dumped his baggage on the deck Hornblower had to make the first advance.

"Are you the master of this vessel, sir?" he asked.

"Captain Baddlestone, master of the hoy *Princess.*"

"I am Captain Hornblower, and I am to be given a passage to England," said Hornblower. He deliberately chose that form of words, nettled as he was by Baddlestone's offhand manner.

"You have your warrant?"

The question and the way in which it was asked rather pricked the bubble of Hornblower's dignity, but he was roused sufficiently by now to feel he would stand no more insolence.

"I have," he declared.

Baddlestone had a large, round, red face, inclining even to purple; from out of it, from under two thick black eyebrows, two surprisingly bright blue eyes met Hornblower's haughty stare. Hornblower was determined to yield not an inch, and was prepared to continue to meet the head-on assault of those blue eyes indefinitely, but he found his flank neatly turned.

"Cabin food a guinea a day. Or you can compound for the passage for three guineas," announced Baddlestone.

It was a surprise to find he had to pay for his subsistence, and Hornblower knew his surprise was apparent in his expression, but he would not allow it to be apparent in his words. He would not even condescend to ask the questions that were on the tip of his tongue. He could be quite sure that Baddlestone had legality on his side. The Navy Office charter of the hoy presumably compelled Baddlestone to give passages to transient officers, but omitted all reference to subsistence. He thought quickly.

"Three guineas, then," he said as loftily as he could, with all the manner of a man to whom the difference between one guinea and three was of no concern. It was not until after he had said the words that he worked out in his mind the deduction that the wind was likely to back round easterly and make a long return passage probable.

During this conversation one pump had been working most irregularly, and now the other one came to a stop; the cessation of the monotonous noise was quite striking. Now Bush was hailing from the *Hotspur*.

"That's only nineteen ton! We can take two more."

"And two more you won't get," yelled Baddlestone in reply. "We're sucked dry."

It was a strange feeling that this was of no concern to Hornblower; he was free of responsibility, even though his mind automatically worked out that *Hotspur* now had fresh water for forty days. It was Meadows who would have to plan to conserve that supply. And with the wind likely to come easterly, *Hotspur* would have to close the mouth of the Goulet as closely as possible—that was Meadows's concern and nothing to do with him, not ever again.

The hands who had been working at the pumps went scuttling back over the gangplank; the two hands from the *Princess* who had been standing by the hoses came back on board dragging their charges. Last came the *Princess's* mate.

"Stand by the lines, there!" yelled Baddlestone. "Jib halliards, Mister!"

Baddlestone himself went to the wheel, and he made a neat job of getting the hoy away from the *Hotspur's* side.

He continued to steer the ship while the half dozen hands under the supervision of the mate set about the task of lifting and stowing the fend-offs that hung along her side. It was only a matter of seconds before the gap between the two ships was too wide to bridge by voice. Hornblower looked across the sparkling water. It appeared that Meadows was summoning all hands in order to address them in an inaugural speech; certainly no one spared a further glance towards the hoy or towards Hornblower standing lonely on the deck. The bonds of naval friendship, of naval intimacy, were exceedingly strong, but they could be ruptured in a flash. It was more than likely that he would never see Bush again.

II

LIFE in the water-hoy *Princess* was exceedingly uncomfortable. She was empty of her cargo of drinking
water, and there was almost nothing to replace it; the
empty casks were too precious to be contaminated by
sea water for use as ballast, and only a few bags of sand
could be squeezed between the empty casks to confer any
stability on her hull. She had been designed with this very
difficulty in view, the lines of her dish-shaped hull being
such that even when riding light her broad beam made her
hard to capsize; but she did everything short of that. Her
motion was violent and, to the uninitiated, quite unpredictable, and she was hardly more weatherly than a raft, sag-
ging off to leeward in a spineless fashion that boded ill for
any prospect of working up to Plymouth while any easterly component prevailed in the wind.

Hornblower was forced to endure considerable hardship. For two days he lingered on the verge of seasick-
ness as a result of this new motion beneath his feet. He
was not actually sick, having had several uninterrupted
weeks at sea already, but he told himself that it would be
less unpleasant if that were to happen—although in his
heart of hearts he knew that was not true. He was

allotted a hammock in a compartment six feet square and five feet high; he at least had it to himself and could derive some small comfort from observing that there were arrangements for eight hammocks, in two tiers of four, to be slung there. It had been a long time since he slept in a hammock, and his spine was slow to adjust to the necessary curvature, while the extravagant leaps and rolls of the hoy made the memory of his cot in *Hotspur* nostalgically luxurious.

The wind stayed northeasterly, bringing clear skies and sunshine but no comfort to Hornblower, save that it was soon evident that he would be eating Baddlestone's "cabin food" for more than three days—a doubtful source of satisfaction. All he wished to do was to make his way to England, to London, to Whitehall, and to secure his posting as captain before anything could happen to interfere. He watched morosely as the *Princess* lost more and more distance to leeward, more even than the clumsy ships of the line clustered off Ushant. There was nothing to read on board, there was nothing to do, and there was nowhere comfortable where he could do that nothing.

He was coming up through the hatchway, weary of his hammock, when he saw Baddlestone whip his telescope to his eye and stare to windward.

"Here they come!" said Baddlestone, unusually communicative. With the greatest possible condescension he passed the telescope over to Hornblower; there could be no more generous gesture (as Hornblower well knew) than for a captain to part with his glass even for a moment when something of interest was in sight.

It was a veritable fleet bearing down on them, something far more than a mere squadron. Four frigates, with every stitch of canvas spread, were racing to take the lead; behind them followed two columns of line-of-battle ships, seven in one and six in the other. They were already setting studding sails as they edged into station. With the wind right astern and all sail set they hurtled down upon the *Princess*. It was a magnificent sight, the commission pennants whipping out ahead, the ensigns flying forward as if in emulation. Under each bluff bow a creamy bow wave mounted and sank as the ships drove on over the blue water. Here was England's naval might seen to its best advantage. The right central frigate came cutting close beside the wallowing water-hoy.

"*Diamond,* thirty-two," said Baddlestone; he had recovered his telescope.

Hornblower stared enviously and longingly at her as she passed within long cannon shot. He saw a rush of men up the foremast rigging. The fore topgallant sail was taken in and reset in the brief space while the *Diamond* was passing. A smart ship that—Hornblower had not detected anything wrong with the set of the sail. The mate of the hoy had just managed to hoist a dirty old red ensign in time to dip it in salute, and the *Diamond's* blue ensign dipped in reply. Now came the starboard column of ships of the line, a three-decker in the lead, towering over the waves, her three rows of chequered gunports revealing themselves as she approached, a blue vice admiral's flag blowing from her fore topgallant mast.

"*Prince of Wales,* ninety-eight. Vice Admiral Sir Robert Calder," said Baddlestone. "There's two other flags with this lot."

The ensigns dipped in salute and the next of the line came on, plunging before the wind with the spray flying. The flags dipped time and again as the seven ships hurtled by.

"A fair wind for Finisterre," said Baddlestone.

"That looks like their course," said Hornblower.

It seemed obvious that Baddlestone knew as much about fleet movements as Hornblower himself, and perhaps even more. Less than a week earlier, Baddlestone had been in Plymouth, with English newspapers to read and all the chatter of the alehouses to listen to. Hornblower himself had heard a good deal of circumstantial gossip from the *Shetland,* the victualler which had come alongside *Hotspur* a couple of days before the *Princess.* The fact that Baddlestone suggested that Calder's destination was merely Finisterre, and not the Straits or the West Indies was almost convincing proof of the extent of Baddlestone's knowledge. Hornblower asked a testing question.

"Heading for the Strait's mouth, do you think?"

Baddlestone eyed him with a trace of pity.

"No farther than Finisterre," he vouchsafed.

"But why?"

Baddlestone found it clearly hard to believe that Hornblower could be ignorant of what was being discussed throughout the fleet and the dockyard.

"Villain-noove," he said.

That was Villeneuve, the French admiral commanding the fleet that had broken out of the Mediterranean some weeks before and fled across the Atlantic to the West Indies.

"What about him?" asked Hornblower.

"He's heading back again, making for Brest. Going to pick up the French fleet there, so Boney thinks. Then the Channel. Boney's army's waiting at Boulong, and Boney thinks he'll eat his next dish of frogs in Windsor Castle."

"Where's Nelson?" demanded Hornblower.

"Hot on Villain-noove's trail. If Nelson don't catch him, Calder will. Boney's going to wait a long time before he sees French tops'ls in the Channel."

"How do you know this?"

"Sloop came in from Nelson while I was waiting for a wind in Plymouth. The whole town knew in half an hour, bless you."

This was the most vital and the most recent information imaginable, and yet it was common knowledge. Bonaparte had a quarter of a million men—trained, equipped, ready—at Boulogne. Transporting them across the Channel in the thousands of flat-bottomed boats that crowded the French Channel ports would be difficult—but with twenty, thirty, possibly forty French and Spanish ships of the line to cover the crossing, it might be achieved. In a month Bonaparte might well be eating frogs in Windsor Castle. The destiny of the world, the fate of civilisation, depended on the concerted movements of the British fleets. If so much was known in

Plymouth last week, it would be known in Bonaparte's headquarters today; detailed knowledge of the British fleet movements was vital for the French in executing what appeared to be essentially a plan of evasion.

Baddlestone was watching him curiously; Hornblower must have allowed some of his emotions to show in his expression.

"No good ever came of worrying," said Baddlestone, and now it was Hornblower's turn to return the sharp gaze.

Until this conversation the pair of them had not exchanged twenty words during this two days of waiting for a wind. Baddlestone apparently cherished hard feelings towards naval officers; maybe Hornblower's refusal to make any advances towards intimacy had softened them.

"Worry?" said Hornblower bravely. "Why should I worry? We'll deal with Boney when the time comes."

Already Baddlestone seemed to regret his voluntary loquacity. As every captain should while on deck, he had been darting repeated glances at the leech of the mainsail and now he rounded on the helmsman.

"Watch what you're doing, blast you!" he roared. "Keep her full and bye! D'ye want us to end up in Spain? An empty water-hoy and a ham-fisted no-seaman at the wheel letting her box the compass!"

Hornblower drifted away during this tirade. His feelings were agitated by apprehensions additional to those Baddlestone had aroused. Here was the crisis of the naval war approaching; there were battles to be fought—and he had no ship. All he had was a promise of one, a promise of being "made post" when he could call upon the Admiralty to redeem that promise. He had endured two years of hardship and danger, monotony and strain, in the blockade of Brest, and now, at the very moment when the war was reaching a climax, he was unemployed. He would be falling between two stools—the battle might well be fought, the crisis over, before he could get to sea again. Calder might intercept Villeneuve within the week, or Bonaparte might be attempting his crossing within a fortnight. Cornwallis's gesture of naming Hornblower for promotion after his long service as captain of *Hotspur* had been a generous one, but at this moment— Better to be a mere commander, addressed as captain by courtesy only, with a ship of his own than to be an ungazetted captain without one. It was enough to drive a man perfectly frantic—and for the last two days the wind had blown steadily from the northeast, keeping him a prisoner in this accursed hoy, while allowing every opportunity to Meadows in the *Hotspur* to distinguish himself. After ten years of experience, Hornblower knew he should have more sense than to fret himself into a fever over winds, the uncontrollable, unpredictable winds that had governed his life since boyhood. But here he was fretting himself into a fever.

III

HORNBLOWER was still in his hammock even
though it was long after daybreak, even though it
was full dawn. He had turned himself over without
waking himself up too much—something he had had to
relearn now that he was sleeping in a hammock again—
and he was determined upon staying where he was, as
somnolent as possible, for the longest possible time. In
that way he would find the day shorter; his mind,
clogged with sleep, would not be working at high tension for so long. Yesterday had been a bad day, when a
favourable slant of wind at nightfall had endured just
long enough to return the *Princess* to the heart of the
blockading squadron before reversing itself maddeningly.

A certain amount of bustle and excitement became
audible on the deck over his head, and there was a boat
alongside. He snarled to himself and prepared to roll out
of his hammock. It would be some trifle of no concern to
him, most likely, but it was sufficient to put an end to his
resolution to stay in his hammock.

He had his feet on deck while still sitting in the hammock when the midshipman appeared. Hornblower glowered at him with bleared eyes, observing the trim white breeches and buckled shoes; this must be some pampered pet from a flagship, and he was offering him a letter. Hornblower was instantly fully awake. He broke the wafer that sealed the note.

> You are hereby requested and required to attend as a witness, at your peril, upon the court martial to be held at nine in the forenoon of this twentieth day of May 1805 in the Cabin of H.M.S. *Hibernia* to try Captain James Percival Meadows, the officers and ship's company of H.M.'s late sloop *Hotspur* for the loss of the said vessel by stranding during the night of the eighteenth day of May 1805.

> HENRY BOWDEN, R. A., *Captain of the Fleet*
> N.B. A boat will be sent.

Here was something startling, astonishing; Hornblower gaped at the note while re-reading it, until he remembered the presence of the midshipman and the consequent need to appear imperturbable.

"Very well, thank you," he snapped. The midshipman had hardly turned his back before Hornblower was dragging out his sea-chest and trying to make up his mind as to how he could get the creases out of his threadbare full-dress coat.

H.M.'s *late* sloop! That could only mean that *Hotspur* was a total loss. But Meadows was alive, which implied that few, if any, lives had been lost. Certainly Meadows had wasted no time in putting *Hotspur* ashore. That would be the easiest thing in the world to do, as no one could say with more certainty than he who had never done it.

To shave he had to drag his sea chest under the hatchway and stand on it with his head protruding through the hatch and his mirror propped up on the maindeck. He was not quite tall enough to dispense with the sea-chest; it crossed his mind that Meadows must have been tall enough to see clear over the coaming without taking steps to add a cubit to his stature.

Baddlestone came up and actually volunteered information as Hornblower stood there balancing precariously; *Princess's* antics made it difficult to use one hand to pull his skin tight while wielding the razor with the other.

"So *Hotspur's* lost on the Black Rock," said Baddlestone.

"I knew she was aground," said Hornblower. "But I didn't know where."

"Do you call being at the bottom of the sea aground? She touched on a falling tide. Holed herself and filled and then rolled off on the flood."

It was remarkable how the fleet auxiliaries picked up the news.

"Any loss of life?" asked Hornblower.

"None that I've heard of," said Baddlestone.

He would certainly have heard if any officers had been

drowned. So they were all safe, including Bush. Hornblower could devote special attention to the tricky area round the left corner of his mouth.

"Giving evidence, I hear?" asked Baddlestone.

"Yes." Hornblower had no desire at all to add to Baddlestone's store of gossip.

"If the wind backs westerly I'll sail without you. I'll put your chest ashore at Plymouth."

"You are exceedingly kind," said Hornblower, and then checked himself. There was nothing to be gained by a quarrel with a man of an inferior social order, and there were other considerations. Hornblower wiped off his face and his razor, pausing to meet Baddlestone's eyes.

"Not many men would have given that answer," said Baddlestone.

"Not many men need their breakfast as much as I do at present," answered Hornblower.

At eight o'clock the boat was alongside, and Hornblower went down into it, wearing the single epaulette on his left shoulder that indicated he had not yet been confirmed in his promotion to captain, and at his side he wore the brass-hilted Langer which was all he could boast as a sword. But he was received with the appropriate ceremony as he went up *Hibernia's* side, following two handsomely turned-out captains with epaulettes on both shoulders who were obviously going to be members of the court. Over on the lee side of the quarterdeck he caught a glimpse of Meadows and Bush, pacing up and down deep in conversation. But the midshipman who was his guide led him away; that was proof (if any were needed) that he was being summoned as an expert witness at the request of the court, and had to be kept away from the defendants to prevent all possibility of either collusion or prejudice.

It was twenty-five minutes after the firing of the gun that indicated the opening of the court when Hornblower was called into the great cabin, where seven captains glittered at a table under the stern windows. Over at one side sat Meadows and Bush, with Prowse, the sailing-master, and Wise, the boatswain. It was distasteful, distressing, uncomfortable, to see the anxiety on those faces.

"The court wishes to address a few questions to you, Captain Hornblower," said the central figure at the table. "Later you may be asked by the defendants to explain your answers."

"Yes, sir," said Hornblower.

"You handed over command of the sloop *Hotspur* in the forenoon of the seventeenth, I understand?"

"Yes, sir."

"Her material condition was good?"

"Reasonably so, sir." He had to speak the truth.

"By that do you mean in good condition or bad?"

"Good, sir."

"The compass deviation card was accurate as far as you were aware?"

"Yes, sir." He could not possibly admit to any carelessness on that subject.

"You have heard that H.M.S. *Hotspur* went aground

23

on the Black Rock with a falling tide. Have you any comments to make, Captain?"

Hornblower set his teeth.

"It would be an easy thing to do."

"Perhaps you would be good enough to elaborate on that statement, Captain?"

There was plenty he could say, but he had to be careful how he said it. He must not appear to be a windbag. He must lay all necessary stress on the navigational difficulties and yet at the same time he must not rate himself too highly for having so long evaded them. He must do all he could for the defendants but he must not overplay his hand. At least there were certain obvious points he could make; they could be instantly confirmed by a glance at the ship's logs.

Hornblower talked about the steady westerly wind which had prevailed for some days earlier, and then about the brisk easterly wind which had sprung up that afternoon. In those conditions the ebbtide could be unpredictably fierce. There was likely at the same time to be a disturbing back eddy inside the rocks which could upset all calculations; the current might reverse itself in a cable's length. From the Black Rock a long reef extended to the southeastward; except at the very tip, breakers were only visible at low water of spring tides; the lead gave no warning of this reef. It would be in no way remarkable for a ship keeping close up to the Goulet to be trapped here.

"Thank you, Captain," said the president when Hornblower had finished, and he glanced over to the defendants. "Have you any questions?"

The president's manner indicated that he thought none could be needed, but Meadows rose to his feet. He seemed to be wasted away; perhaps the borrowed clothes he was wearing contributed to the effect, but he was hollow-eyed and his cheeks seemed sunken, the left one twitching at intervals.

"Captain," he asked. "The wind was northeasterly and brisk?"

"It was."

"The best conditions for a sortie by the French?"

"Yes."

"What was *Hotspur's* proper station in those conditions?"

"As close up to the Goulet as possible."

It was a good point that had needed accentuation.

"Thank you, Captain," said Meadows, sitting down, and Hornblower looked to the president for permission to retire.

But Meadows's question had given rise to another.

"Would you kindly tell the court, Captain," asked the president, "how long you commanded the *Hotspur* on blockade service?"

"A little over two years, sir." That was the literal answer that had to be given.

"And how much of that time were you close up to the Goulet? A rough estimate is all that is needed, Captain."

"I suppose half the time—one third of the time."

"Thank you, Captain." It was a point tending very much to discount the one Meadows had made. "You may now retire, Captain Hornblower."

He could glance over at Bush and the others, but it had to be a glance of complete indifference; he must not prejudice the court by a display of sympathy. He made his bow and withdrew.

IV

I T WAS less than half an hour after Hornblower returned to the *Princess* that Baddlestone got the news,
passed from one auxiliary vessel to another as they wallowed, waiting for a wind.

"Guilty," said Baddlestone, turning to Hornblower.

This was one of the moments when Hornblower was
most in need of an appearance of stolidity while finding
the greatest difficulty in attaining it.

"What about the sentence?" he asked. Tension gave
his voice a grating sound which he hoped would be
interpreted as harsh indifference.

"Reprimand," said Baddlestone, and Hornblower felt
the relief flooding his vitals.

"What kind of a reprimand?"

"Just a reprimand."

Not a severe reprimand, then. After a "guilty" verdict
it was the mildest sentence a court-martial could pro-
nounce, save for mere admonishment. But with *Hotspur*
lost, every officer and warrant officer in the ship would
have to apply for re-employment, and the powers-that-be
might still have a word to say. Unless they were vindic-
tive, however, there could be little danger to anyone except possibly Meadows. It was only then that Baddlestone

doled out another fragment of information which would have saved Hornblower anxiety.

"They cleared the first lieutenant and the sailing-master," he said. Hornblower kept his mouth shut, determined to give no hint of his feelings.

Baddlestone had the telescope to his eye now, and Hornblower followed his gaze. A ship's longboat under two balance lugsails was running before the wind in their general direction; it took no more than a glance for Hornblower to identify her as belonging to a ship of the line, and as far as he could judge from her foreshortened length she was of the largest size, belonging to a three-decker, likely enough.

"More company, I'll lay guineas to shillings," said Baddlestone, the telescope still clamped to his eye.

Hornblower's fingers fluttered with the yearning to use the telescope.

"Yes," went on Baddlestone, retaining it with a cruelty possibly unconscious. "It looks like it."

He turned to bellow orders for the hanging of fend-offs on the starboard side, and to bring the hoy to the wind to provide a slight lee on that side. Then there was no need for the telescope; Hornblower with the naked eye could recognise Bush sitting bare-headed in the stern-sheets, and then Meadows beside him. On the next thwart forward were the warrant officers of the late *Hotspur,* and forward of them was a jumble of figures he could not identify.

The longboat surged round into the wind and came neatly alongside.

"Boat ahoy!" hailed Baddlestone.

"Party with warrants for passage," came Bush's voice in reply. "We're coming aboard."

Baddlestone gobbled inarticulately for a second or two at this absence of a "by your leave," but already the longboat had hooked on. At once it became obvious how violently the hoy rolled; the longboat was stable by comparison. There was a moment's delay before Meadows hauled himself onto the hoy's deck, and a further delay before Bush appeared behind him. Hornblower hurried forward to make them welcome; it was obvious that with the loss of the *Hotspur* her officers were being returned to England for other appointments, while presumably the crew had been distributed round the ships of the squadron.

It was only with an effort that Hornblower brought himself to address Meadows first.

"Glad to see you again, Captain Meadows," he said. "And you too, Mr. Bush."

Bush had a half smile for him, but not Meadows; he was under the shadow of a reprimand. Baddlestone watched the encounter with as much cynical amusement as his bulging red face could convey.

"Perhaps you gentlemen will be good enough to show me your warrants," he said.

Bush thrust his hand into his breast pocket and produced a sheaf of papers.

"Fourteen if you count them," he replied. "And these are ratings I'm not responsible for."

"You'll be at pretty close quarters," said Baddlestone.

"Cabin food a guinea a day, or you can compound for three guineas for the passage."

Meadows entered into the conversation not with a word, but with a gesture. He turned a bleak gaze and looked behind him. The warrant officers had begun to arrive on deck. Prowse the master, Cargill and the other mates, Huffnell the purser, the boatswain and sailmaker and carpenter and cooper and cook. They were followed by a number of ratings. One of them turned to help another on board, and Hornblower saw that this man had lost a hand at the wrist, presumably in one of the numerous shipboard accidents that eroded the crews of the blockading fleet. Several more men succeeded him. The reason for their return to England was not immediately apparent. Most of them were in all probability ruptured so badly as to rate discharge; possibly one or two others may have been illegally impressed and fortunate enough to have friends at home with sufficient influence to win their freedom. Altogether it was a large and formidable body of men mustered on the deck of the hoy, crowding it, while the longboat cast off and, with her lugsails hauled as flat as boards, set off on the long beat back to the flagship.

"By the terms of your contract you victual ratings at sixpence a day," said Meadows. "This voyage you'll victual officers at the same rate, and that's all it's worth."

Baddlestone followed Meadows's gaze and ran his eye over the crowd, and Meadows accentuated his earlier glance with a wave of his hand. Hornblower was reminded of the legendary captain of a ship of war who, when asked for his authority for some particular action, pointed to his guns and said, "There!"

"Is this piracy?" exclaimed Baddlestone.

"Call it anything you like," answered Meadows.

Baddlestone fell back a step or two, staring round him, to find no comfort in sea or sky, and the longboat several cable lengths away. Meadows's expression was unchanging, bleak and lonely. Whatever had been the terms of the reprimand he had received, he obviously felt it severely. Believing himself to be a man without a future, he could well be careless about any possible charge of mutiny Baddlestone could bring against him. His officers were sheltered under his authority; they had lost all they possessed when *Hotspur* sank, and they also knew that by law they had gone on half pay from that moment. They could be dangerous men, and the ratings would obey them without hesitation. The *Princess's* crew in addition to Baddlestone comprised a mate, a cook, four hands and a boy; the odds were overwhelming, with no chance of appealing to higher authority, and Baddlestone realised it even though his words still conveyed defiance.

"I'll see you in the dock, Mr. Captain Meadows," he said.

"Captain Hornblower travels at the same rate," said Meadows imperturbably.

"I've paid my three guineas," interposed Hornblower.

"Better still. That'll be—a hundred and twenty-six sixpences already paid. Am I right, Mr. Baddlestone?"

V

IN THE *Princess,* conditions were intolerably crowded. Where Hornblower's hammock had been slung there were now seven more, so that each of the eight officers occupied no more space than might be found inside a coffin. They were packed together in two tiers of four, in an almost solid mass, but not quite solid; as the *Princess* leaped and bounded there was just enough play for everyone to bump against his neighbor or against a bulkhead, maddeningly, every second or two. Hornblower in the lower tier (which he had sensibly selected to avoid the poisonous upper air) had Meadows above him, a bulkhead on one side and Bush on the other. Sometimes the weight of the three bodies to his left compressed him against the bulkhead, and sometimes he swayed the other way and thumped Bush in the ribs; sometimes the deck below rose up to meet him and sometimes Meadows's vast bulk above came down to impress itself on him—Meadows was an inch or two longer than the cabin and lay in a pronounced curve. Hornblower's restless mind deduced that these latter contacts were proof of how much the *Princess* "worked"—the cabin was pulled out of shape when she rolled, diminishing its height by an inch or two, as was confirmed by the creaking and crackling that went on all round him. Long before midnight Hornblower wriggled with difficulty out of his hammock and then, snaking along on his back under the lower tier, crawled out of the cabin to where the purer air outside fluttered his shirttails.

After the first night, common sense dictated another arrangement whereby the passengers, officers and ratings alike, slept "watch and watch," four hours in bed and four hours squatting in sheltered corners on deck. It was a system to which they were all inured, and was extended, naturally and perforce, to cooking and meals and every other activity. Even so, the *Princess* was not a happy ship. The passengers were likely to snarl at each other at small provocation, and potential trouble on a far greater scale was only a hair's breadth away, as the experts with whom the hoy swarmed criticised Baddlestone's handling of her. For the persistent summer breezes still blew from between north and east, and she lost distance to leeward in a manner perfectly infuriating to men who for months and years had not seen homeland or family. That wind meant sparkling and delightful weather; it might mean a splendid harvest in England; but it meant irritation in the *Princess*. Bitter arguments developed between those who advocated that Baddlestone should reach to the westward, into the Atlantic, in the hope of finding a favourable slant of wind there, and those who still had sufficient patience to recommend beating about where they were—but both schools were ready to agree that the trim of the sails, the

33

handling of the helm, the course set when under way, and the tack selected when lying to could and should be improved upon.

Hope came timourously to life one noontime; there had been disappointments before, and hardly a soul dared speak a word when, after a period of almost imperceptible easterly airs, something a trifle more vigorous awoke, with a hint of south in it, backing and strengthening so that the sheets could be hauled in. Baddlestone bellowed at the hands, and the motion of the *Princess* changed from spiritless wallowing to a flat-footed advance, an ungainly movement over the waves like a cart horse trying to canter over wet furrow.

"What's her course, d'you think?" asked Hornblower.

"Nor'east, sir," said Bush, tentatively, but Prowse shook his head as his natural pessimism asserted itself.

"Nor'east by east, sir," he said.

"A trifle of north in it, anyway," said Hornblower.

Such a course would bring them no nearer Plymouth, but it might give them a better chance of catching a westerly slant outside the mouth of the Channel.

"She's making a lot of leeway," said Prowse, gloomily, his glance sweeping round from the set of the sails to the barely perceptible wake.

"We can always hope," said Hornblower. "Look at those clouds building up. We've seen nothing like that for days."

"Hope's cheap enough, sir," said Prowse gloomily.

Hornblower looked over towards Meadows, standing at the mainmast. His face bore that bleak expression still

34

unchanged; he stood solitary in a crowd, yet even he was impelled to study wake and sail-trim and rudder, until Hornblower's gaze drew his glance and he looked over at them, hardly seeing them.

"I'd give something to know what the glass is doing," said Bush. "Maybe it's dropping, sir."

"Shouldn't be surprised," said Hornblower.

He could remember so acutely running for Tor Bay in a howling gale. Now Maria was in Plymouth, and the second child was on the way.

Prowse cleared his throat; he spoke unwillingly, because he had something cheerful to say.

"Wind's still veering, sir," he said at length.

"Freshening a trifle, too, I fancy," said Hornblower. "Something may come of this."

In these latitudes at this time of year heavy weather was likely when the wind veered instead of backing, when it swung towards south from northeast, when it freshened, and when dark clouds began to build up as they were doing at the moment. The mate was marking up the traverse board.

"What's the course, Mister?" asked Hornblower.

"Nor' by east half north."

"Just another point or two's all we need," said Bush.

"Got to give Ushant a wide berth anyway," said Prowse.

Even on this course they were actually lessening the distance that lay between them and Plymouth; it was in a quite unimportant fashion, but it was a comforting thought. The horizon was closing in on them a little with the diminishing visibility. There was still a sail or two in sight, all towards the east, for no vessel made as much leeway as the *Princess*. But it was indication of the vastness of the ocean that there were so few sails visible although they were in the immediate vicinity of the Channel Fleet.

Here came a much stronger gust of wind, putting the *Princess* over on her lee side with men and movables cascading across the deck until the helmsman allowed her to pay off a point.

"She steers like a dray," commented Bush.

"Like a wooden piggin," said Hornblower. "Sideways as easily as forwards."

It was better when the wind veered still further round, and then came the moment when Bush struck one fist into the palm of the other hand.

"We're running a point free!" he exclaimed.

That meant everything in the world. It meant that they were not on a compromise course where as much might be lost as gained. It meant that they were steering a course direct for Plymouth, or as direct as Baddlestone's calculations could indicate; if they were correct, leeway had now become a source of profit instead of loss. It meant that the wind was a trifle on the *Princess's* quarter, and that would almost certainly be her best point of sailing, considering her shape. It meant that they were getting finally clear of the coast of France. Soon they would be well in the mouth of the Channel with considerable freedom of action. Finally it had to be repeated that they were running free, a fantastic, marvellous change for men who had endured for so long the depressing alternatives of lying to or sailing close-hauled.

Someone near at hand raised his voice; Hornblower could tell that he was not hailing, or quarrelling, but singing, going through an incomprehensible and purposeless exercise for the sake of some strange pleasure it gave. "From Ushant to Scilly is thirty-five leagues . . ." That was perfectly true, and Hornblower supposed that circumstances justified making this sort of noise about it. He steeled himself to a stoical endurance as others joined in: "Farewell and adieu to you, Spanish ladies!" It was very noticeable that the atmosphere in the *Princess* had changed metaphorically as well as actually; spirits had risen with the fall in the barometer. There were smiles, there were grins to be seen. With the wind veering another couple of points, as it did, there was a decided probability that the evening of the next day would see them into Plymouth. As if she had caught the prevailing infection, the *Princess* began to leap over the waves; in her clumsiness there was something almost lewd, like a tubby old lady showing her legs in a drunken attempt to dance.

Yet Meadows, still standing at the mainmast, did not share in the mirth and the excitement. He looked isolated and unhappy; even the two officers who had been next senior to him in the *Hotspur*—his first lieutenant and his sailing-master—were over here chatting with Hornblower instead of keeping him company. Hornblower began to make his way over to him, and at that moment a rain squall came hurtling down upon the

Princess, causing sudden confusion as the weaker spirits rushed forward and aft for shelter.

"Plymouth tomorrow, sir," said Hornblower conversationally when he reached Meadows's side.

"No doubt, sir," said Meadows.

"We're in for a bit of a blow, I think," said Hornblower, gazing upwards into the rain. He knew he was being exaggerated in the casual manner he was trying to adopt, but he could not modify it.

"Maybe," said Meadows.

"Likely enough we'll have to make for Tor Bay instead," suggested Hornblower.

"Likely enough," agreed Meadows—although agreement was too strong a word for that stony indifference.

Hornblower would not admit defeat yet. He struggled on trying to make conversation, feeling a little noble— more than a little—at standing here growing wet to the skin in an endeavour to relieve another man's troubles. It was some small comfort when the rain squall passed on over the *Princess's* lee bow, but it was a much greater relief when one of the seamen forward hailed loudly.

"Sail ho! Two points on the weather bow!"

Meadows came out of his apathy sufficiently to look forward along with Hornblower in the direction indicated. With the sudden clearing of the weather the vessel was no more than hull-down at this moment of sighting, no more than five or six miles away and in plain view, close-hauled on the port tack on the *Princess's* starboard bow, on a course that would apparently come close to intercepting the course of the *Princess* within the hour.

"Brig," commented Hornblower, making the obvious conversational remark, but he said no more as his eye recorded the other features that made themselves apparent.

There was that equality between the fore and main topmasts; there was that white sheen about her canvas; there was even something about the spacing of those masts—everything was both significant and dangerous. Hornblower felt Meadows's hand clamp round his arm like a ring of iron.

"Frenchman!" said Meadows, with a string of oaths.

"May well be," said Hornblower.

The spread of her yards made it almost certain that she was a ship of war, but even so there was a considerable chance that she was British, one of the innumerable prizes captured from the French and taken into the service recently enough to have undergone little alteration.

"Don't like the looks of her!" said Meadows.

"Where's Baddlestone?" exclaimed Hornblower, turning to look aft.

He tore himself from Meadows's grasp when he perceived Baddlestone, newly arrived on deck, with his telescope trained on the brig; the two of them at once started to push towards him.

"Come about, damn you!" yelled Meadows, but at that very same second Baddlestone had begun to bellow orders. There was a second or two of wild and dangerous confusion as the idle passengers attempted to aid, but they were all trained seamen. With the sheets hauled in against the violent pressure of the wind, the helm was put over. *Princess* gybed neatly enough; the big lugsails flapped thunderously for a moment and then as the sheets were eased off she lay over close-hauled on the port tack. As she did so, she lifted momentarily on a wave and Hornblower, his eyes still on the brig, saw the latter lift and heel at the same time. For half a second—long enough—he could see a line of gunports, the concluding fragment of evidence that she was a ship of war.

Now *Princess* and brig were close-hauled on the same tack, with the brig on *Princess's* quarter. Despite the advantage of her fore-and-aft rig it seemed that *Princess* lay a trifle farther off the wind than did the brig. She was nothing like as weatherly, and far slower; the brig would headreach and weather on her. Hornblower's calculating eye told him that it would be only a question of hours before *Princess* would sag down right into the brig's gaping jaws; should the wind veer any farther the process would be accelerated.

"Take a pull on that foresheet," ordered Meadows, but before he could be obeyed, the hands he addressed were checked by a shout from Baddlestone.

"Avast there!" Baddlestone turned on Meadows. "I command this ship and don't you meddle!"

The barrel-shaped merchant captain stood with his hands belligerently on his hips. Meadows turned to Hornblower.

"Do we have to put up with this, Captain Hornblower?" he asked.

"Yes," replied Hornblower.

That was the legal position. Fighting men and naval officers though they were, they were only passengers, subject to the captain's command. Even if it should come to a fight, that rule held good; by the laws of war a merchant ship was entitled to defend herself, and in that case the captain would still be in command, as he would be in going about or laying a course or in any other matter of ship handling.

"Well, I'm damned!" said Meadows.

Hornblower might not have answered quite so sharply and definitely if his curious mind had not taken note of one particular phenomenon. Just before Meadows had issued his order, Hornblower had been entranced in close observation of the relative trim of the two big lugsails. They were sheeted in at slightly different angles, inefficiently to the inexperienced eye. Analysis of the complicated—and desperately interesting—problem in mechanics suggested that the setting was correct; with one sail slightly diverting the wind towards the other, the best results could be expected with the sails as they were trimmed at present. Hornblower had been familiar with the fascinating problem ever since as a midshipman he had had charge of a ship's longboat. Meadows must have forgotten about it, or never studied it; his action would have slightly cut down their speed. Baddlestone could be expected to know how to get the best out of a ship he had long commanded and a rig he had sailed in all his life.

"There's her colours," said Baddlestone. "Frenchy, of course."

"One of those new fast brigs they've been building,"

said Hornblower. "Bricks, they call 'em. Worth two of ours."

"Are you going to fight her?" demanded Meadows.

"I'm going to run as long as I can," answered Baddlestone.

That was obviously the only thing to do.

"Two hours before dark. Nearer three," said Hornblower. "Maybe we'll be able to get away in a rain squall."

"Once he gets up to us—" said Baddlestone, and left the sentence unfinished. The French guns could pound the hoy to pieces at close range; the slaughter in the crowded little craft would be horrible.

They all three turned to stare at the brig. She had gained on them perceptibly already, but all the same . . .

"It'll be pretty well dark before she's in range," said Hornblower. "We've a chance."

"Small enough," said Meadows. "Oh, God—"

"D'ye think I want to rot in a French gaol?" burst out Baddlestone. "All I have is this hoy. Wife and children'll starve."

What about Maria, with one child born and another on the way? And—and—what about that promised post rank? Who would lift a finger for a forgotten almost-captain in a French prison?

Meadows emitted a stream of senseless oaths.

"We've thirty men," said Hornblower. "They won't think we've more than half a dozen—"

"By God, we could board her!" exclaimed Meadows, the oaths ending abruptly.

Could they? Could they get alongside? No French captain in his right mind would allow it, would risk damage to his precious ship in the strong breeze that was blowing. A spin of the brig's wheel at the last moment, an order to luff, and *Princess* would have missed her chance; a salvo of grape and the *Princess* would be a wreck. Moreover, an unsuccessful attempt would convey its own warning—the French captain and the French crew could anticipate trouble. The brig would have a crew of ninety at least, most likely more; unless there was total surprise, thirty men would not have a chance against them. And Hornblower's vivid imagination conjured up a mental picture of the *Princess,* alongside the brig and rolling wildly as she undoubtedly would. There could be no wild rush; the thirty-odd men would reach the brig's deck in twos and threes, without a chance. It would have to be complete, total surprise to stand the slightest chance of success.

With these considerations racing through his mind, Hornblower looked from Meadows to Baddlestone, watching their expressions change from momentary excitement and hope to uneasy doubt. Something else came up in his mind that called for rapid action, and he turned away to bellow in his loudest and most penetrating voice to the groups clustered about the deck.

"Get down out of sight, all of you! I don't want a single man to show himself! Get down out of sight!"

He turned back to meet a stony gaze from both Baddlestone and Meadows.

"I thought we'd better not show our hand until it's

43

played out," he said. "With a glass the brig'll soon be able to see we're crowded with men, and it might be as well if she didn't know."

"I'm the senior," snapped Meadows. "If anyone gives orders it's me."

"Sir—" began Hornblower.

"Commander, May eighteen hundred," said Meadows. "You're not in the *Gazette* yet. You've not read yourself in."

It was an important point, a decisive point. Hornblower's appointment as commander dated back only to April 1803. Until his promised captaincy was actually official, he must come under Meadows's orders. That was something of a setback. His polite attempts at conversation earlier with Meadows must have appeared as deferential currying for favour instead of the generous condescension he had intended. And it was irritating not to have thought of all this before. But that irritation was nothing compared with that roused by the realisation that he was a junior officer again, forced to proffer advice instead of giving orders—and this after two years of practically independent command. It was a pill to swallow; oddly, as the metaphor occurred to him, he was actually swallowing hard to contain his annoyance, and the coincidence diverted him sufficiently to cut off the angry answer he might have made. They were all three of them tense, even explosive. A quarrel among them might well be the quickest way to a French prison.

"Of course, sir," said Hornblower, and went on—if a thing was worth doing it was worth doing well—"I must beg your pardon. It was most thoughtless of me."

"Granted," said Meadows, only slightly grudgingly.

It was easy enough to change the subject—a glance towards the brig set the other two swinging round to look as well.

"Still headreaching on us, blast her!" said Baddlestone. "Weathering on us, too."

Obviously she was nearer, yet the bearing was unchanged; the chase would end with the brig close up to the *Princess* without any alteration in course—and the infuriating corollary was that any other action the *Princess* might take would only shorten the chase.

"We've no colours hoisted," said Meadows.

"Not yet," replied Baddlestone.

Hornblower caught his eye and stared hard at him. It was inadvisable to speak or even for Hornblower to shake his head, even a trifle, but somehow the message reached Baddlestone.

"No need to hoist 'em yet," Baddlestone went on. "It leaves our hands free."

There was not the least chance that the Frenchman would take the *Princess* to be anything other than a fleet auxiliary, but still . . . There was no need to take the smallest action that might commit them. Things looked differently in a report, or even in a ship's log. If the Frenchman tired of the chase, or was diverted somehow from it, it would be well to offer him a loophole excusing him; he could say he believed the *Princess* to be a Dane or a Bremener. And until the colours had been hoisted and hauled down again, *Princess* was free to take any action that might become possible.

"It's going to be dark before long," said Hornblower.

"She'll be right up to us by then," snarled Meadows, and the oaths streamed from his mouth as ever. "Cornered like rats."

That was a good description; they were cornered, hemmed in by the invisible wall of the wind. Their only line of retreat was in the direction of the brig, and the brig was advancing remorselessly up that line. If the *Princess* was a rat, the brig was a man striding forward, club in hand. And being cornered meant that even in darkness there would be no room to escape, no room for any evasive manoeuvre, right under the guns of the brig. But, like a rat, they might still fly at their assailant with the courage of desperation.

"I wish to God," said Meadows, "we'd run down on her when we sighted her. And my damned sword and pistols are at the bottom of the sea. What arms d'you have on board?"

Baddlestone listed the pitiful contents of the arms chest; even a water-hoy carried cutlasses and pistols for defence against hostile rowing boats, which were well known to push out from the French shore to snap up unarmed prizes in a calm.

"We could get a few more," interposed Hornblower. "They're bound to send a boat and a prize crew. And in the dark—."

"By God, you're right!" shouted Meadows, and he turned on Baddlestone. "Don't hoist those colours! We'll get out of this! By God, we'll take her!"

"We could try," said Baddlestone.

"And by God, I'm the senior naval officer!" said Meadows.

A man returning to England under a cloud would be rehabilitated almost automatically if he brought a prize in with him. Meadows might possibly reach the captains' list before Hornblower.

"Come on," said Meadows. "Let's get the hands told off."

They were entering upon the wildest, the most reckless enterprise that could be imagined, but they were desperate men. Hornblower himself was desperate, although he told himself during the bustle of preparation that he was a man under orders with no alternative except to obey. He would not go so far as to point out to himself that they were carrying out the plan he himself had devised —and on which he would have acted, danger or no danger, had he been in command.

VI

PRINCESS was lying hove-to in the darkness. The mere fact of being hove-to could be construed by the enemy as an admission of surrender. From her forestay flickered a lighted lantern, trimmed right down, a tiny dot of light that would give the brig little chance to observe what was going on in the waist of the hoy. Across the total blackness a cable length to leeward, four bright lanterns revealed both the brig's position and the fact that she was lowering a longboat.

"They're coming," growled Meadows, crouching at the gunwale. "Remember, cold steel." In the strong breeze that was blowing, confused noises would pass unnoticed, but a shot would be heard clearly enough downwind.

Now the crouching men could see a solid mass tossing in the darkness; now they could hear the grind of oars; now they could hear French voices. Hornblower was waiting. His was the only white face in the hoy; the others were painted black. He threw them a line as they hooked on.

"*Montez*," he said; it was an effort to keep his voice from cracking with excitement.

Princess was heaving on the agitated sea in as lively a fashion as ever. It was several seconds before the first

Frenchman boarded, cutlass and pistols at his belt, a midshipman arriving to take possession of the prize. Hornblower heard the dull thump when they struck him down. He was disposed of before the next man could make the leap. So was the next man, and the next, and the next. It was all horribly, repulsively easy to men who were prepared to be utterly ruthless.

Hornblower from his point of vantage could just determine when the last man had boarded; he could see that the oarsmen were preparing to hand up the prize crew's gear.

"Right!" he called sharply.

Meadows and his allocated group were crouched and ready; they hurled themselves down into the boat, a torrent of falling bodies. An oar clattered and rattled; Hornblower could hear belaying pins striking against skulls. There was one astonished outcry, and no more. Hornblower could not hear the dead or unconscious bodies being dropped into the sea, but he knew that was being done.

"We've arms for seven," came Meadows's voice. "Come on, longboat party. Hornblower, get started."

There had been two hours in which to organise the attack; everybody knew what part he had to play. Hornblower ran aft and a group of almost invisible black-faced figures loomed up at his side. He dipped his hand into the paint bucket that stood ready and hastily smeared his forehead and cheeks before making the next move. The hoy's boat was in tow under the quarter; they hauled it in and scrambled down.

"Cast off!" said Hornblower, and a desperate shove with the port-side oars got them clear. "Easy all!"

Tiller in hand, Hornblower stared through the darkness from under the stern of the hoy. It had taken time to man the brig's longboat; only now was it beginning to head back to the brig. As it rose on a wave Hornblower caught sight of it silhouetted against the light from the brig's lanterns. He must wait for several more seconds; if the brig's crew were to see two boats returning where one had set out, the alarm might well be given.

It was a bad business that the French boat's crew had all been dropped into the sea; necessary act of war or not, the French could say they had been murdered. They would give no quarter to any survivors on the brig's deck if the attack were to fail; the approaching battle would be victory or death, with no compromise possible.

There was the longboat approaching the brig's side, clearly visible in the light of the lanterns.

"Give way, port side!" The boat swung round as the oars bit. "Give way, starboard side!"

The boat began to move through the water, and the tiller under Hornblower's hand came to life. He set his course; there was no need to call upon the oarsmen to pull with all their strength; they were well aware of the situation. Hornblower was reminded of something he had read somewhere, a fragment of English history about a Saxon over-king who, in token of his preeminence, had been rowed on the river Dee by eight under-kings. Most of the oars in this boat were being pulled by officers—Bush was pulling bow oar starboard side, seconding the efforts of Wise the boatswain and Wallis the surgeon and two or three master's mates, and the master and purser and gunner were packed in among the seamen. The boat was crammed with men and low in the water, but every fighting man was needed.

The brig's lanterns grew steadily nearer, with still no sound of trouble; the brig was expecting the return of her longboat, and would suspect nothing until it was actually alongside. It was unlikely that the rushes from the two small boats could be launched simultaneously—thereby confronting the French crew in a flash by thirty furious enemies where they had looked for half a dozen friends—but it was possible.

There it was. A pistol shot, the sound coming up-wind. More shots. It had been settled that Meadows's party should use their pistols as soon as they reached the deck. It would be necessary to shock and bewilder the surprised Frenchmen and get them into a panic; the arrival of a boarding party firing pistols would be a likely means to bring this about.

"Easy all! Bow-man!"

The hoy's boat surged alongside the brig, under her forechains; an outburst of yells and screams on deck indicated where Meadows was fighting. A dozen hands reached for the shrouds, Hornblower's among them. It was a miracle the boat did not capsize—warrant officers would be as harebrained and excitable as young seamen when the occasion was desperate.

"Go on!" yelled Hornblower. To the devil with formality; these were not men who needed leading.

The boat lightened as the black-faced mob sprang up into the chains, Hornblower the fifth or sixth to reach the deck. There was no opposition, even though there were many figures rushing about the dimly lighted deck.

They were beside the hatchway now, and a white-faced figure was just emerging, waist level with the deck. A black-faced figure swung an axe; the Frenchman tumbled down again.

Now a running figure cannoned into Hornblower and flung him aside, nearly knocking him off his feet. But he was in no immediate danger; the hurrying Frenchman was intent only on flinging himself bodily down the hatchway. He was followed by a dozen other panic-stricken figures, a terrified herd pursued by two cutlass-swinging men with black faces. When the rush ended, Hornblower leaned over the hatchway and fired his pistol down into the mass below; that was probably the most effective use for the single round which was all he had, for it would scare away from the hatchway those other Frenchmen who were trying to ascend.

"Get the hatch cover on!" said Hornblower. "Wise, get it battened down! Master's mates, stay with Wise. Others follow me!"

He hurried aft, his brass-hilted Langer in his hand. Two or three distracted figures came rushing forward. They had white faces, and they were struck down. Hornblower suddenly remembered to yell; if there were any real opposition aft, it would be likely to dissolve at the sound of a hostile battle cry from the rear. He saw a sudden rectangle of light, and a white figure—white shirt, white breeches, white face—coming through it. It was the French captain emerging from his cabin, and he was met by a huge figure rushing at him with raised cutlass. Hornblower saw the French captain with arm extended in the classic lunge; he saw the cutlass come whirling down; then both figures tumbled out of sight.

The battle, if such it could be called, was almost over. The Frenchmen, unarmed, taken utterly by surprise, could do nothing except to try to save their lives. But every figure with a white face was hunted round the deck to be slaughtered pitilessly by men mad with excitement, except for one group of Frenchmen who flung themselves grovelling on the deck screaming for mercy —the killing of two of them sated the bloodlust and the survivors were hustled into a corner by the taffrail. Hornblower had a feeling that a few men had dashed up the rigging and were sheltering there; they could be dealt with later.

He looked round the deck. The eerie illumination afforded by the lanterns swinging in the shrouds was increased at regular intervals by the light from the cabin door, a light which came and went as the door swayed open and shut with the rolling of the ship. The deck was littered with corpses, grotesque and horrible. Was that a dead man coming to life? Someone recovering consciousness? Certainly it was a body heaving upward, but in a way no living man would get to his feet. Anything was possible in these hideous surroundings. No! That man was dead and being shoved up from below. He must have fallen across the after scuttle and the crew below the deck was getting him out of the way. As Hornblower looked, the dead body rolled and fell with a thump onto the deck and there was the scuttle with two hands uplifted through it. Hornblower leaped, slashing with his sword, and the hands disappeared to the accompaniment of a yell from below. Hornblower drew the sliding cover across and shot the bolt.

Hornblower straightened up to find himself face to face with someone who had come forward to take the same precaution, and involuntarily he tightened his grip on his sword hilt—he was not ready for a black face so close to his.

"We've settled it," said Baddlestone's voice.

"Where's Meadows?" croaked Hornblower, his throat still dry with tension.

"He's a goner," answered Baddlestone, with a wave of his arm.

The cabin door swung open again as if in response, throwing an arc of light over the deck, and Hornblower remembered. On the far side of the scuttle lay two corpses. That one must be Meadows, lying half on his side, arms and legs asprawl. Standing out from his chest was the handle of a rapier, and two feet of the blade stuck out through his back. In the black face the teeth shone whitely, as Meadows had bared them in the ferocity of his attack; in the swaying lights his lips seemed still to be going through contortions of rage. Beyond him lay the French captain in white shirt and breeches, but where face and head should be there was only something horrible. On the deck lay the cutlass which had dealt the shattering blow, delivered in one final explosion of Meadows's vast strength as the French rapier went through his heart. Years ago the émigré nobleman who had given Hornblower fencing lessons had spoken of the *coup des deux veuves*—the reckless attack that made two widows—and here was an example of it.

"Any orders, sir?" Here was Bush recalling him to reality.

"Ask Captain Baddlestone," replied Hornblower.

A touch of formality would clear the nightmares from his mind. At the same instant something else occurred to remind him that action was still demanded. A crashing sound and a jarring shock beneath his feet told him that the Frenchmen below were battering at the scuttle. From forward there came similar noises, and a voice hailed, "Cap'n, sir! They're tryin' to bash up the hatch cover!"

"There was a whole watch below when we boarded," said Baddlestone.

Of course, that would help to account for the comparative ease of the victory—thirty armed men attacking fifty men surprised and unarmed. But it meant that at least another fifty enemies were below and refusing to be subdued.

"Get for'rard and deal with it, Bush," said Hornblower—it was only when Bush had departed that Hornblower realised that he had omitted the vital "Mr." He must be quite unstrung.

"We can keep 'em down all right," said Baddlestone.

It would hardly be possible for the men below to force their way to the deck through a hatchway or scuttle efficiently guarded, even if the covers were pounded to fragments as seemed to be happening at the moment. But to maintain guards every moment, over the scuttle and the hatchway and the prisoners aft by the taffrail, and at the same time to provide crews to handle the brig and the *Princess* would mean a good deal of strain.

The light was playing strange tricks; the unmanned wheel seemed to be turning of its own volition. Hornblower stepped across to it. There was not the easy feel to it which might be expected with the ship hove-to; then, suddenly, it spun free.

"They've cut the tiller ropes down below," he reported to Baddlestone.

At that moment a sledgehammer blow against the underside of the deck made them leap in surprise. Hornblower felt his feet tingling from the violent impact.

"What the devil—?"

There was another enormous blow, and, staring down, Hornblower could see a tiny glimmer of light some inches from his right foot—a small jagged hole had appeared there.

"Come away!" he said to Baddlestone, and they retreated to the scuppers. "They're firing muskets down there!"

A one-ounce musket ball fired at a range of no more than an inch or two would strike the deck with the force of twenty sledgehammers; it would pierce the planking with sufficient velocity to shatter a leg or take a life.

"They guessed there'd be someone standing near the wheel," said Baddlestone.

Splintering crashes forward made it clear that the Frenchmen were destroying the hatch cover there, and now there began a similar noise from the scuttle aft; it sounded as if they had found an axe down below and were using it.

"It's not going to be easy to sail her home," said Baddlestone, turning an inquiring gaze on Hornblower.

"If they won't surrender, it's going to be damned difficult," said Hornblower.

Often when the deck of a ship was carried by a rush, the survivors down below were demoralised sufficiently to yield, but should they determine on resistance the situation became complicated, especially when, as in the present case, the numbers below were far greater than the numbers above and were apparently being led by someone of energy and courage. Hornblower had often envisaged such a situation, but even his imagination had not pictured musket balls being fired up through the deck.

"Even if we get the brig underway," he said, "there's the relieving tackles—"

"And hell to pay," said Baddlestone.

By adroit handling of the sails, it was possible, after a fashion, to steer a ship whose rudder was useless. But down below there were the relieving tackles, and half a dozen sturdy men heaving on them could drag the rudder round, not merely nullifying the efforts of the men on deck but actually imperilling the ship by laying her unexpectedly aback.

"We'll have to bolt for it," said Hornblower; it was an

irritating, an infuriating suggestion to have to make, and Baddlestone reacted with a string of oaths.

"No doubt you're right," he said grudgingly. "Ten thousand pounds apiece in prize money—gone! We'll burn her—set her on fire before we go!"

"We can't do that!" Hornblower's reply was jerked from him even before he had time to think.

Fire in a wooden ship was the deadliest of enemies; if they left the brig well alight no efforts by the Frenchmen left behind could extinguish the flames. Fifty, perhaps sixty or seventy, Frenchmen would burn to death if they did not leap overboard to drown. Hornblower could not do it in cold blood; the alternative was already forming in his mind.

"We can leave her a wreck," he said. "Cut the jeers, cut the halliards—cut the forestay, for that matter! Five minutes' work, and it'll take 'em the best part of a day before they can get sail on her again."

Perhaps it was the appeal to the demon of destruction that made up Baddlestone's mind for him.

"Come on!" he said. "Let's get to work."

The project called for only the smallest amount of organisation; the men they commanded were many of them trained officers who could grasp the situation with the briefest explanation. There were plenty of men to mount guard at the scuttle and at the hatch (whose cover was rapidly disintegrating under the force of axe blows from beneath) while the men who were to wreak destruction were assigned and sent about their tasks. The turmoil had already begun before Hornblower remembered one of the important duties of a King's officer in a captured ship—a flash of clarity that pierced like lightning through the sombre cloud that oppressed his mind.

He dashed into the French captain's cabin. There stood the captain's desk, and as he should have expected, it was locked. He fetched a handspike from the nearest gun, and it was only a minute's work with the aid of its powerful leverage to wrench the desk open. There were the ship's papers, letter book and fair log and all. And there was something unusual, too, something flat, rectangular, and heavy—a sheet of lead bound with tarred twine. A further glance showed that it was actually a sandwich of lead, with papers enclosed. Undoubtedly those papers were unusually important; dispatches, probably, or additions and changes to the signal book. The leaden casing told its own story; the package was to be thrown overboard if the ship was in danger of capture, but the French captain had been killed before he could take this emergency action.

A tremendous crash outside on the deck told him that the work of dismantling the brig was proceeding. He looked round him and dragged a blanket from the cot, dumped all the ship's papers into it, and twisted the blanket into a bag which he slung over his shoulder as he hurried out. The crash had been caused by the fall of the mainyard, as a result of the cutting of the jeers. It lay across the deck in a tangle of rigging, which did not obscure the fact that the fall had sprung it—half-broken it—in the centre. Five minutes' work by a gang of men who knew exactly what to do had left the brig a wreck.

Forward, Baddlestone and several other men were on guard over the hatchway. The frantic Frenchmen below were still battering at it with axes, and already a jagged hole was visible.

"We've fired every shot we have down at 'em," said Baddlestone. "When we go we'll have to run for it!"

His words were underlined by a blast from below, and a musket bullet sang through the air between him and Hornblower.

"Wish we had—" began Baddlestone, and suddenly stopped. An idea had occurred to him, and in the same instant it struck Hornblower as well.

When the brig, just at darkness, had closed up on the *Princess,* it had fired a shot across her bows. The gun that fired that shot would almost certainly be ready for action. Baddlestone rushed over to one battery, Hornblower to the other.

"There's a charge here!" yelled Baddlestone. "Here, Jenkins, Sansome! Bear a hand!"

Hornblower searched along the shot-garlands and found what he sought.

"It's canister that'll do the trick," he said, bringing it over to Baddlestone and the others, who were working like madmen to swing the gun around and point it at the hatchway. It called for vast effort; the trucks of the carriage groaned and shrieked as they scraped sideways on the deck. Baddlestone took the powder charge in its serge bag from the carrying bucket which had stood by the gun. The charge was rammed home, and then against it the canister—a cylinder of thin metal containing a hundred and fifty bullets. Gurney, the gunner, pierced the serge bag through the touch hole with the pricker, and primed with fine powder from the horn. Then he began to force in the quoin, the wedge that caused the breech of the gun to rise so that the muzzle pointed with infinite menace down the hatchway. Baddlestone glowered round, turning his black face this way and that.

"Get down in the boats, all of you!" he said.

"I'd better stay with you," said Hornblower.

"Get down into your boat with your party!" shouted Baddlestone.

It was the sensible thing to do; this was a rear-guard action, and the covering force should be reduced to the absolute minimum. Hornblower herded his party down into the *Princess's* boat, and most of Baddlestone's men went down into the brig's. Hornblower stood for a moment on tiptoe, with the sea surging round, holding on to the forechains with one hand while the other still retained its grip on the blanket-bundle of books. He could just see from the longboat; there was the swaying deck, with the dead men tumbled over it and the incredible confusion of the dismantling. Two lanterns still burned in the shrouds, and the light from the cabin still waxed and waned with the swinging of the door.

Gurney had forced a second quoin under the breech of the gun, so that it pointed down at a steep angle into the hatchway. He and Baddlestone stood clear, and then he jerked at the lanyard. A bellowing roar, a blinding flash, a billow of smoke; yells and screams from down below, distinctly heard where Hornblower was standing. Then the Englishmen came running across the deck: Baddle- stone and Gurney, the guards at the scuttle and the hatchway, the guards over the prisoners. Hornblower watched them scrambling down into the boat, Baddle- stone last, turning to yell defiance before he disappeared down into his boat. Hornblower released his hold on the chains and sat down in the sternsheets.

"Shove off!" he said.

A tiny pinpoint of dancing light showed where *Princess* still lay to. In five minutes they would be under way again, free from pursuit, with the wind fair for Plymouth.

VII

HORNBLOWER wrote the final lines of his letter, rapidly checked it through, from "My dear Wife," to "Your loving husband, Horatio Hornblower," and folded the sheet and put it in his pocket before going up on deck. The last turn was being taken round the last bollard, and *Princess* was safely alongside the quay in the victualling yard in Plymouth.

As always, there was something unreal, a sort of nightmare clarity in this first contact with England. The people, the sheds, the houses, seemed to stand out with unnatural sharpness; voices sounded different with the land to echo them; the wind was vastly changed from the wind he knew at sea. The *Princess's* passengers were already stepping ashore, and a crowd of curious onlookers had assembled; the arrival of a water-hoy from the Channel Fleet was of interest enough because she might have news, but a water-hoy which had actually captured, and for a few minutes had held possession of, a French brig of war was something very new.

There were farewells to say to Baddlestone; besides making arrangements to land his sea-chest and ditty bag there was something else to discuss.

"I have the French ship's papers here," said Horn-blower, indicating the bundle.

"What of them?" countered Baddlestone.

"It's your duty to hand them over to the authorities," said Hornblower. "In fact I'm sure you're legally bound to do that. Certainly as a King's officer I must see that is done."

Baddlestone seemed to be in a reserved mood. "Then why not do it?" he said at length, after a long hard look at Hornblower.

"It's a prize of war and you're the captain."

Baddlestone voiced his contempt for prizes of war that consisted solely of worthless papers.

"You'd better do it, Captain Hornblower," he said, after his oaths and obscenities had subsided. "They'll be worth something to you."

"They certainly may be," agreed Hornblower.

Baddlestone's reserve was replaced now by a look of inquiring puzzlement. He was studying Hornblower as if seeking some hidden motive behind the obvious ones.

"It was you who thought of taking the papers," he said, "and you're ready to hand them over to me?"

"Of course. You're the captain."

Baddlestone shook his head slowly as if he was giving up a problem; but what the problem was Hornblower never did discover.

Now, as he stepped ashore, there was the strange sensation of feeling the unmoving earth under his feet; there was the silence that fell on the two groups of passengers

—officers and ratings—as he approached them. He had to take a formal farewell of them—it was only thirty hours since he and they had fought their way along the French brig's deck, swinging their cutlasses. There was a brotherhood in arms—one might almost say a brotherhood of blood—between them, something that divided them off sharply into a caste utterly different from the ignorant civilians here.

But the very first thing to deal with on shore was his letter. There was a skinny and barefooted urchin hanging on the fringe of the crowd.

"You, boy!" called Hornblower. "D'you want to earn a shilling?"

"Iss, that do I." The homely accent was accompanied by an embarrassed grin.

"D'you know Driver's Alley?"

"Iss, sir."

"Here's sixpence and a letter. Run all the way and take this letter to Mrs. Hornblower. Can you remember that name? Let's hear you say it. Very well. She'll give you the other sixpence when you give her the letter. Now—run!"

Now for the good-byes.

"I said good-bye to most of you gentlemen only a few days back, and now I have to do so again. And a good deal has happened since then."

"Yes, sir!" an emphatic agreement, voiced by Bush as the only commissioned officer present.

"Now I'm saying good-bye once more. I said before

that I hoped we'd meet again, and I say it now. And I say 'thank you,' too. You know I mean both of those things."

"It's us that have to thank you, sir," said Bush, through the inarticulate murmurs uttered by the officers.

"Good-bye, you men," said Hornblower to the other group. "Good luck."

"Good-bye and good luck, sir."

He turned away. There was a dockyard labourer available to wheel away his gear on a barrow, on which he could also lay the blanket-bundle which swung from his hand; the precious papers would not be out of his sight, and he had his dignity as a captain to consider. That dignity Hornblower felt imperilled enough as it was by the difficulty he experienced in walking like a landsman; the cobbles over which he was making his way seemed as if they could not remain level. He knew he was rolling in his gait like any Jack Tar, and yet, try as he would, he could not check the tendency while the solid earth seemed to seesaw under his feet.

The labourer, as might have been expected, had no knowledge of where the admiral commanding the port was to be found; he did not know even his name, and a passing clerk had to be stopped and questioned.

"The port admiral?" The lard-faced clerk who repeated Hornblower's words was haughty, and Hornblower was battered and dishevelled, his hair long and tousled, his clothes rumpled, all as might be expected after nearly two weeks of crowded life in a water-hoy. But there was an epaulette, albeit a shabby one, on his left shoulder, and when the clerk noticed it he added a faint, "Sir."

"Yes, the port admiral."

"You'll find him in his office in the store building over there."

"Thank you. Do you know his name?"

"Foster. Rear Admiral Harry Foster."

"Thank you."

That must be Dreadnought Foster. He had been one of the board of captains who had examined Hornblower for Lieutenant all those years ago in Gibraltar, the night the Spaniards sent the fireships in.

The marine sentry at the outer gate presented arms to the epaulette, but he was not so wooden as to allow to pass unnoticed the blanket-bundle that Hornblower took from the labourer; his eyes swivelled round to stare at it even while his neck stayed rigid. Hornblower took off his battered hat to return the salute and passed through. The flag lieutenant who interviewed him next noticed the bundle as well, but his expression softened when Hornblower explained he was carrying captured documents.

"From the *Guêpe,* sir?" asked the lieutenant.

"Yes," answered Hornblower in surprise.

"The Admiral will see you, sir."

It was only yesterday, when Hornblower had examined the log more carefully in the hoy, that he had discovered the French brig's name. It was only an hour ago that the *Princess* had made contact with the land, and yet the story was already known in the admiral's office.

At least it would save a little time; Maria would be waiting at the dockyard gate.

Dreadnought Foster was just as Hornblower remembered him—swarthy, with an expression of sardonic humour. Luckily he appeared to have no recollection of the nervous midshipman whose examination had been fortunately interrupted that evening in Gibraltar. Like his flag lieutenant he already had heard something of the story of the capture of the brig—one more example of the speed with which gossip can fly—and he grasped the details, as Hornblower supplied them, with professional ease.

"And those are the documents?" he asked, when Hornblower reached that point in his sketchy narrative.

"Yes, sir."

Foster reached out a large hand for them.

"Not everyone would have remembered to bring them away, Captain," he said, as he began to turn them over. "Log. Day book. Station bill. Quarter bill. Victualling returns."

He had noticed the lead-covered dispatch first of all, naturally, but he had laid it aside to examine last.

"Now what do we have here?" He studied the label. "What does 'S.E.' mean?"

"Son Excellence—His Excellency, sir."

"His Excellency the Captain General of—what's this, Captain?"

"Windward Isles, sir."

"I might have guessed that, seeing it says 'Martinique,' " admitted Foster. "But I never had a head for French. Now—"

He fingered the penknife on his desk. He studied the tarred twine that bound the leaden sandwich. Then he put the knife down reluctantly and looked up at Hornblower.

"I don't think I'd better meddle," he said. "This'll be best left for Their Lordships."

Hornblower had had the same thought although he had not ventured to voice it. Foster was looking at him searchingly.

"You intend going to London, of course, Captain?" he said.

"Yes, sir."

"Naturally. You want a ship, I think."

"Yes, sir. Admiral Cornwallis named me for promotion last month."

"Well. This—" Foster tapped the dispatch. "This will save you time and money. Flags!"

"Sir!" The flag lieutenant was instantly in attendance.

"Captain Hornblower will need a post-chaise."

"Aye aye, sir."

"Have it at the gate immediately."

"Aye aye, sir."

"Have a travel warrant made out for London."

"Aye aye, sir."

Foster turned his attention once more to Hornblower and smiled sardonically at the bewilderment and surprise he saw in his face. For once, Hornblower had been caught off his guard and had allowed his emotions to show.

"Seventeen guineas that will cost King George, God bless him," said Foster. "Aren't you grateful for his bounty?"

Hornblower had regained control over himself; he was even able to conceal his irritation at his lapse.

"Of course, sir," he said, in almost an even tone and with an expressionless face.

"Every day—ten times a day sometimes," said Foster, "I have officers coming in here, even admirals, trying to get travel warrants to London. The excuses I've heard! And here you don't care."

"Of course I'm delighted, sir," said Hornblower. "And greatly obliged, too."

Maria would be waiting at the gate, but under Foster's sardonic gaze he was too proud to show any further weakness. A King's officer had his duty to do. And it was less than three months since he had last seen Maria; some officers had been parted from their wives since the outbreak of war more than two years ago.

"No need to be obliged to me," said Foster. "This is what decided me." "This" was of course the dispatch, which he tapped again.

"Yes, sir."

"Their Lordships should find it worth seventeen guineas. I'm not doing it for your sweet sake."

"Naturally, sir."

"Oh yes, and I'd better give you a note to Marsden. It will get you past the doorkeeper."

"Thank you, sir."

Those last two speeches—Hornblower digested them while Foster scribbled away at the letter—were hardly tactful when considered in relation to each other. They implied a certain lack of charm on Hornblower's part. Marsden was Secretary to the Lords of the Admiralty, and the suggestion that Hornblower needed a note to gain admittance was an unexpressed but disparaging comment on his appearance.

"Chaise will be at the gates, sir," announced the flag lieutenant.

"Very well." Foster sanded his letter and poured the sand back into the caster, folded the letter and addressed it, sanded it once more, and once more returned the sand. "Seal that, if you please."

As the flag lieutenant busied himself with candle and wax and seal, Foster folded his hands and looked over again at Hornblower.

"You're going to be pestered for news at every relay," he said. "The country can't think about anything except 'What's Nelson doing?' and 'Has Boney crossed yet?' They'll discuss Villain-noove and Calder the way they used to discuss Tom Cribb and Jem Belcher."

"Indeed, sir? I fear I know nothing about them." Tom Cribb and Jem Belcher were disputing the heavyweight championship of England.

"Just as well."

"Ready, sir," said the flag lieutenant, handing the sealed letter to Hornblower, who held it for an embarrassed second before putting it in his pocket—it seemed rather cavalier treatment for a dispatch to the Secretary of the Admiralty.

"Goodbye, Captain," said Foster, "and a pleasant journey."

"I've had your baggage put in the chaise, sir," said the flag lieutenant on the way to the gate.

"Thank you," said Hornblower.

Outside the gate there was the usual small crowd—labourers waiting to be hired, anxious wives, and mere sightseers. Their attention was at this moment taken up by the post-chaise which stood waiting with the postillion at the horses' heads.

"Well, goodbye, sir, and a pleasant journey," said the flag lieutenant, handing over the blanket-bundle.

From outside the gate came a well-remembered voice. "Horry! Horry!"

There stood Maria by the wicket-gate, in bonnet and shawl, with little Horatio in her arms.

"That's my wife and my child," said Hornblower abruptly. "Goodbye, sir." He strode out through the gate and found himself clasping Maria and the child in the same embrace.

"Horry, darling. My precious," said Maria. "You're back again. Here's your son—look how he's growing up. He runs about all day long. There, smile at your daddy, poppet."

Little Horatio did indeed smile, for a fleeting instant, before hiding his face in Maria's bosom.

"He looks well indeed," said Hornblower. "And how about you, my dear?"

He stood back to look her over. There was no visible sign at present of her pregnancy, except perhaps in the expression in her face.

"To see you is to give me new life, my loved one," said Maria.

It was painful to realise that what she said was so close to the truth. And it was horribly painful to know that he had next to tell her that he was leaving her in this very moment of meeting.

Already, and inevitably, Maria had put out her right hand to twitch at his coat, while holding little Horatio in her left arm.

"Your clothes look poorly, Horry darling," she said. "How crumpled this coat is. I'd like to get at it with an iron."

"My dear—" said Hornblower. This was the moment to break the news, but Maria anticipated him.

"I know," she said, quickly. "I saw your chest and bag being put into the chaise. You're going away."

"I fear so."

"To London?"

"Yes."

"Not one little moment with me—with us?"

"I fear not, my dear."

Maria was being very brave. She held her head back and looked straight at him unflinchingly; there was just the tiniest quiver of her lips to indicate the stresses within.

"And after that, darling?" asked Maria. When she spoke her tone gave a further hint of those stresses.

73

"I hope to get a ship. I shall be a captain, remember, dear."

"Yes." Just the one word, of heartbroken acquiescence.

Perhaps it was fortunate then that Maria noticed something that distracted her, but Hornblower was inclined to believe that Maria deliberately and bravely distracted herself. She lifted her hand to his cheek, to his jawbone below his left ear.

"What's this?" she asked. "It looks like paint. Black paint. You haven't looked after yourself very well, dear."

"Very likely it's paint," agreed Hornblower.

He had repressed the almost automatic reaction to draw back from a public caress, before he realised what it was that Maria had observed. Now there was a flood of recollection. The night before last, he had stormed onto the deck of the *Guêpe* with a gang of yelling madmen with blackened faces. He had heard cutlass blades crunch on bone, he had heard screams for mercy, he had seen nine pounds of canister fired down into a crowded 'tween-decks. Only the night before last, and here was Maria, simple and innocent and ignorant, and his child, and the staring onlookers, in the English sunshine. It was only a step out of one world into another, but it was a step infinitely long, over a bottomless chasm.

"Horry, darling?" said Maria, inquiringly, and broke the spell.

She was looking at him anxiously, studying him, and frightened by what she saw; he knew he must have been scowling, even snarling, as his expression revealed the emotions he was re-experiencing. It was time to smile.

"It wasn't easy to clean up in *Princess*," he said. It had been hard to apply turpentine to his face before a mirror in the leaping water-hoy with the wind on the quarter.

"You must do it as soon as ever you can," said Maria. She was scrubbing at his jaw with her handkerchief. "It won't come off for me."

"Yes, dear." This was the moment, with reassurance restored to Maria's face, to tear himself from her.

"And now goodbye, dear," he said gently.

"Yes, dear."

She had learned her lesson well during half a dozen farewells since their marriage. She knew that her incomprehensible husband disliked any show of emotion even in private, and disliked it twenty times as much with a third party present. She had learned that he had moments of withdrawal which she should not resent because he was sorry for them afterwards. And above all that, she had learned that she weighed in the scale nothing, nothing at all, against his duty. She knew that if she were to pit herself and her child against this it would only end in a terrible hurt which she could not risk because it would hurt him as much or more.

It was only a few steps to the waiting chaise; Hornblower took note that his sea-chest and ditty bag were under the seat on which he put his precious bundle, and turned back to his wife and child.

"Goodbye, son," he said. Once more he was rewarded with a smile instantly concealed. "Goodbye, my dear. I shall write to you, of course."

She put up her mouth for kissing, but she held herself

75

back from throwing herself into his arms, and she was alert to terminate the kiss at the same moment as he saw fit to withdraw. Hornblower climbed up into the chaise, and sat there, feeling oddly isolated. The postillion mounted and looked back over his shoulder.

"London," said Hornblower.

The horses moved forward and the small crowd of onlookers raised something like a cheer. Then the hoofs clattered on the cobbles and the chaise swung round the corner, abruptly cutting Maria off from his sight.

VIII

"THIS'LL DO," said Hornblower to the landlady.

"Bring it up, 'Arry," yelled the landlady over her shoulder, and Hornblower heard the heavy feet of her dim-witted son on the uncarpeted stairs as he carried up the sea-chest.

There was a bed and a chair and a wash-hand stand and a mirror on the wall; all a man could need. These were the cheap lodgings recommended to him by the last postillion; there had been a certain commotion in the frowsy street when the post-chaise had turned into it from the Westminster Bridge Road and had pulled up outside the house—it was not at all the sort of street where post-chaises were expected. The cries of the children who had been attracted by the sight could still be heard through the narrow window.

"Anything you want?" asked the landlady.

"Hot water," said Hornblower.

The landlady looked a little harder at the man who wanted hot water at nine in the morning.

"Or right. I'll get you some," she said.

Hornblower looked round him at the room; it seemed to his disordered mind that if he were to relax his attention the room would revolve around him on its own. He sat down in the chair; his backside felt as if it were one big bruise, as if it had been beaten with a club. It would have been far more comfortable to stretch out on the bed, but that he dared not do. He kicked off his shoes and wriggled out of his coat, and became aware that he stank.

" 'Ere's your 'ot water," said the landlady, re-entering.
"Thank you."

When the door closed again, Hornblower pulled himself wearily to his feet and took off the rest of his clothes. That was better; he had not had them off for days, and this room was sweltering hot with the June sun blazing down on the roof above. Stupid with fatigue, he more than once had to stop to think what he should do next, as he sought out clean clothing and unrolled his housewife. The face he saw in the mirror was covered with hair on which the dust of travel lay thick, and he turned away from it in disgust.

It was a grisly and awkward business to wash himself inch by inch in the wash basin, but it was restorative in some small degree. Everything he had been wearing was infiltrated with dust, which had penetrated everywhere —some had even seeped into his sea-chest and pattered out when he lifted out his clothes. With his final pint of hot water he applied himself to shave.

That brought about a decided improvement in his appearance, although even now the face that looked out at him from the mirror was drawn very fine, with a pallor that made his tan look as if it were something painted on. He looked closely at his left jaw. Wear and tear as well as the shave had removed the paint that Maria had noticed. He put on clean clothes—of course they were faintly damp, as always when newly come from the sea, and would stay so until he could get them washed in fresh water. Now he was ready; he had consumed exactly the hour he had allowed himself. He picked up his bundle of papers and walked stiffly down the stairs.

He was still incredibly stupid with fatigue. During the last hours in the post-chaise he had nodded off repeatedly while sitting up and lurching over the rutted roads. To travel post-haste had a romantic sound but it was utterly exhausting. When changing horses he had allowed himself sometimes half an hour—ten minutes in which to eat, and twenty in which to doze, with his head pillowed on his arms resting on the table. Better to be a sea officer than a courier, he decided. He paid his halfpenny toll on the bridge; normally he would have been greatly interested in the river traffic below him, but he could not spare it a glance at present. He turned up Whitehall and reached the Admiralty.

Dreadnought Foster had displayed good sense in giving him that note; the doorkeeper eyed Hornblower and his bundle with intense suspicion—it was not only cranks and madmen that he had to turn away, but naval officers who came to pester Their Lordships for employment.

"I have a letter for Mr. Marsden from Admiral Foster," said Hornblower, and was interested to see the doorkeeper's expression soften at once.

"Would you please write a note to that effect on this form, sir?" he asked.

Hornblower wrote "Bringing a message from Rear Admiral Harry Foster" and signed it, along with his boardinghouse address.

"This way, sir," said the doorkeeper. Presumably—certainly, indeed—the Admiral commanding at Plymouth would have the right of immediate access, personally or through an emissary, to Their Lordships' Secretary.

The doorkeeper led Hornblower into a waiting room and bustled off with the note and the letter; in the waiting room there were several officers sitting in attitudes of expectancy or impatience or resignation, and Hornblower exchanged formal good mornings with them before sitting down in a corner of the room. It was a wooden chair, unfriendly to his tormented sitting parts, but it had a high back with wings against which it was comfortable to lean.

Somehow Frenchmen had boarded the *Princess* by surprise, in the darkness. Now they were raging through the little ship, swinging cutlasses. Everything on board was in a turmoil while Hornblower struggled to free himself from his hammock to fight for his life. Someone was shouting "Wake up, sir!" which was the very thing he wanted to do but could not. Then he realised that the words were being shouted into his ear and someone was shaking him by the shoulder. He blinked twice and came back to life and consciousness.

"Mr. Marsden will see you now, sir," said the unfamiliar figure who had awakened him.

"Thank you," replied Hornblower, seizing his bundle and getting stiffly to his feet.

"Fair off you was, sir," said the messenger. "Come this way, sir, please sir."

Hornblower could not remember whether the other individuals waiting were the same as he had first seen or had changed, but they eyed him with envious hostility as he walked out of the room.

Mr. Marsden was a tall and incredibly elegant gentleman of middle age, old-fashioned in that his hair was tied at the back with a ribbon, yet elegant all the same because the style exactly suited him. Hornblower knew him to be already a legendary figure. His name was known throughout England because it was to Marsden that dispatches, which were later printed in the newspapers, were addressed ("Sir, I have the honour to inform you for the further information of Their Lordships that . . ."). First Lords might come and First Lords might go—as Lord Barham had just come and Lord Melville had just gone—and so might Sea Lords, and so might admirals, but Mr. Marsden remained the Secretary. It was he who handled all the executive work of the greatest navy the world had ever seen. Of course he had a large staff—no fewer than forty clerks, so Hornblower had heard—and he had an assistant secretary, Mr. Barrow, who was almost as well known as he was, but even so out of everybody in the world Mr. Marsden could most nearly be described as the one who was fighting single-handed the war to the death against the French Empire and Bonaparte.

It was a lovely, elegant room looking out onto the Horse Guards parade, a room that exactly suited Mr. Marsden, who was seated at an oval table. At his shoulder stood an elderly clerk, grey-haired and lean, of an obviously junior grade, to judge by his threadbare coat and frayed linen.

Only the briefest salutations were exchanged while Hornblower put his bundle down on the table.

"See what there is here, Dorsey," said Marsden over his shoulder to the clerk, and then, to Hornblower, "How did these come into your possession?"

Hornblower told of the momentary capture of the *Guêpe;* Mr. Marsden kept his grey eyes steadily on Hornblower's face during the brief narrative.

"The French captain was killed?" asked Marsden.

"Yes." There was no need to tell about what Meadows's cutlass had done to the French captain's head.

"That indicates that this may be genuine," decided Marsden, and Hornblower was puzzled momentarily, until he realised that Marsden meant that there had been no *ruse de guerre* and that the papers had not been deliberately "planted" on him.

"Quite genuine, I think, sir. You see—" he said, and went on to point out that the French brig could not have expected for one moment that the *Princess* would launch a counter-attack on her.

"Yes," agreed Marsden; he was a man of icy-cold

manner, speaking in a tone unchangingly formal. "You must understand that Bonaparte would sacrifice any man's life if he could mislead us in exchange. But, as you say, Captain, these circumstances were completely unpredictable. What have you found, Dorsey?"

"Nothing of great importance except this, sir."

"This" was of course the lead-covered dispatch. Dorsey was looking keenly at the twine which bound up the sandwich.

"That's not the work of Paris," he said. "That was tied in the ship. This label was probably written by the captain, too. Pardon me, sir."

Dorsey reached down and took a penknife from the tray in front of Marsden, and cut the twine, and the sandwich fell apart.

"Ah!" said Dorsey.

It was a large linen envelope, heavily sealed in three places, and Dorsey studied the seals closely before looking over at Hornblower.

"Sir," said Dorsey. "You have brought us something valuable. Very valuable, I should say, sir. This is the first of its kind to come into our possession."

He handed it to Marsden, and tapped the seals with his finger. "Those are the seals of this newfangled Empire of Bonaparte's, sir," he said. "Three good specimens."

More than a year had passed, Hornblower realised, since Bonaparte had proclaimed himself emperor, and the republican Consulate had given place to the Empire. When Marsden permitted him to look closely, he could

see on the seals the imperial eagle with its thunderbolt—
to his mind not quite as dignified a bird as it might be,
for the feathers that sheathed its legs offered a grotesque
impression of trousers.

"I should like to open this carefully, sir," said Dorsey.

"Very well. You may go and attend to it."

Fate hung in the balance for Hornblower at that
moment; and somehow Hornblower was aware of it
with uneasy premonition, while Marsden kept his cold
eyes fixed on his face, apparently as a preliminary to
dismissing him.

Later in his life—even within a month or two—Hornblower could look back in perspective at this moment as
one in which his destiny was diverted in one direction instead of in another, dependent on a single minute's
difference in timing. He was reminded, when he looked
back, of the occasions when musket bullets had missed
him by no more than a foot; a small, a microscopic
correction of aim on the part of the marksman would
have laid Hornblower lifeless, his career at an end.
Similarly, at this moment, a few seconds' delay along the
telegraph route, a minute's dilatoriness on the part of a
messenger, and Hornblower's life would have followed a
different path.

For the door at the end of the room opened abruptly
and another elegant gentleman came striding in. He was
some years younger than Marsden, and dressed soberly
but in the very height of fashion, his lightly starched
collar reaching to his ears, and a white waistcoat picked
out with black calling unobtrusive attention to the slen-

derness of his waist. Marsden looked round with some annoyance at this intrusion, but restrained himself when he saw a sheet of paper fluttering in the intruder's hand.

"Villeneuve's in Ferrol," said the newcomer. "This has just come by telegraph. Calder fought him off Finisterre and was given the slip."

Marsden took the dispatch and read it with care.

"This will be for His Lordship," he said, calmly, rising with deliberation from his chair. Even then he did not noticeably hurry. "Mr. Barrow, this is Captain Hornblower. You had better hear about his recent acquisition."

Marsden went out through a hardly perceptible door behind him, bearing news of the most vital, desperate importance. Villeneuve had more than twenty ships of the line, French and Spanish—ships which could cover Bonaparte's crossing of the Channel—and he had been lost to sight for the last three weeks, since Nelson had pursued him to the West Indies. Calder had been stationed off Finisterre to intercept and destroy him if he tried to slip back to Europe, and Calder had apparently failed in his mission.

"What is this acquisition, Captain?" asked Barrow, the simple question breaking into Hornblower's train of thought like a pistol shot.

"Only a dispatch from Bonaparte, sir," he said. Hornblower used the 'sir' deliberately, despite his confusion; Barrow was, after all, the Second Secretary, and his name was nearly as well known as Marsden's.

"But that may be of vital importance, Captain. What was the purport of it?"

"It is being opened at the present moment, sir. Mr. Dorsey is attending to that."

"I see. Dorsey in forty years in this office has become accustomed to handling captured documents. It is his particular department."

"I fancied so, sir."

There was a moment's pause, while Hornblower braced himself to make the request that was clamouring inside him for release.

"What about this news, sir? What about Villeneuve? Could you tell me, sir?"

"No harm in your knowing," said Barrow. "A gazette will have to be issued as soon as it can be arranged. Calder met Villeneuve off Finisterre. He was in action with him for the best part of two days—it was thick weather—and then they seem to have parted."

"No prizes, sir?"

"Calder seems to have taken a couple of Spaniards."

Two fleets, each of twenty ships or more, had fought for two days with no more result than that. England would be furious—for that matter England might be in very serious peril. The French had probably employed their usual evasive tactics, edging down to leeward with their broadsides fully in action while the British tried to close and paid the price for the attempt.

"And Villeneuve broke through into Ferrol, sir?"

"Yes."

"That's a difficult place to watch," commented Hornblower.

"Do you know Ferrol?" demanded Barrow sharply.

"Fairly well, sir."

"How?"

"I was a prisoner of war there in '97, sir."

"Did you escape?"

"No, sir, they set me free."

"By exchange?"

"No, sir."

"Then why?"

"I helped to save life in a shipwreck."

"You did? So you know about conditions in Ferrol?"

"Fairly well, sir, as I said."

"Indeed. And you say it's a difficult place to watch. Why?"

Sitting in a peaceful office in London, a man could experience as many surprises as on the deck of a frigate at sea. Instead of a white squall suddenly whipping out of an unexpected quarter, or instead of an enemy suddenly appearing on the horizon, here was a question demanding an immediate answer regarding the difficulty of blockading Ferrol. This was a civilian, a landsman, who needed the information, and urgently. For the first time in a century the First Lord was a seaman, an admiral—it would be a feather in the Second Secretary's cap if in the next conference he could display familiarity with conditions in Ferrol.

Hornblower had to express in words what up to that

moment he had only been conscious of as a result of his seaman's instinct. He had to think fast to present an orderly statement.

"First of all it's a matter of distance," he began. "It's not like blockading Brest."

Plymouth would be the base in each case; from Plymouth to Brest was less than fifty leagues, while from Plymouth to Ferrol was nearly two hundred. Communication and supply would be four times as difficult, Hornblower pointed out.

"Even more so with prevailing westerly winds," he added.

"Please go on, Captain," said Barrow.

"But really, that is not as important as the other factors, sir," said Hornblower.

It was easy to go on from there. A fleet blockading Ferrol had no friendly refuge to leeward. A fleet blockading Brest could run to Tor Bay in a westerly tempest —the strategy of the past fifty years had been based on that geographic fact. A fleet blockading Cadiz could rely on the friendly neutrality of Portugal, and had Lisbon on one flank and Gibraltar on the other. Nelson watching Toulon had made use of anchorages on the Sardinian coast. But off Ferrol it would be a different story. Westerly gales would drive a blockading fleet into the cul-de-sac of the Bay of Biscay, whose shores were not merely hostile but wild and steep-to and swept by rain and fog. To keep watch over Villeneuve in Ferrol, particularly in winter, would impose an intolerable strain on the watcher, especially as the exits from Ferrol were far easier and more convenient than the single exit from Brest—the largest imaginable fleet could sortie from Ferrol in a single tide, which no large French fleet had ever succeeded in doing from Brest.

Hornblower recounted what he had observed in Ferrol regarding the facilities for the prompt watering of a fleet, for berthing, for supply; the winds that were favourable for exit and the winds that made exit impossible; the chances of a blockader making furtive contact with the shore—as he himself had done off Brest—and the facilities to maintain close observation over a blockaded force.

"You seem to have made good use of your time in Ferrol, Captain," said Barrow.

Hornblower would have shrugged his shoulders, but restrained himself in time from indulging in so un-English a gesture. The memory of that desperately unhappy time came back to him in a flood and he was momentarily lost in retrospective misery. He came back into the present to find Barrow's eyes still fixed on him with curiosity, and he realised, self-consciously, that for a moment he had allowed Barrow a glimpse into his inner feelings.

"At least I managed to learn to speak a little Spanish," he said; it was an endeavour to bring a trace of frivolity into the conversation, but Barrow continued to treat the subject seriously.

"Many officers would not have taken the trouble," he commented.

Hornblower shied away from this personal conversation like a skittish horse.

"There's another aspect to the question of Ferrol," he said, hurriedly.

"And what is that?"

The town and its facilities as a naval base lay at the far end of long and difficult roads over mountain passes, by way of Betanzos or Villalba. To support a fleet under blockade there, to keep it supplied by road with the hundreds of tons of necessary stores, might be more than the Spaniards could manage.

"You know something of these roads, Captain?"

"I was marched over them when I was a prisoner."

"Boney's emperor now and the dons are his abject slaves. If anyone could compel them to attend to their business it would be Boney."

"That's very likely, sir." This was more a political question than a naval one, and it would be presumption on his part to make further comment.

"So we're back," said Barrow, half to himself, "to where we've been ever since '95, waiting for the enemy to come out and fight, and in your opinion, Captain, we're in a worse situation than usual."

"That's only my opinion, sir," said Hornblower hastily. These were questions for admirals, and it was not healthy for junior officers to become involved in them.

"If only Calder had thrashed Villeneuve thoroughly!" went on Barrow. "Half our troubles would be over."

Hornblower had to make some reply or other, and he had to think fast for noncommittal words that would not imply a criticism of an admiral by a junior officer.

"Just possibly, sir," he said.

He knew that as soon as the news of the battle of Cape Finisterre was released the British public would boil with rage. At Camperdown, at the Nile, and at Copenhagen victories of annihilation had been gained. The mob would never be satisfied with this mere skirmish, especially with Bonaparte's army poised for embarkation on the Channel coast and Britain's fate dependent on the efficient handling of her fleets. Calder might well experience the fate of Byng; he could be accused, like Byng, of not having done his utmost to destroy the enemy. A political upheaval might easily occur in the near future.

That led to the next thought; a political upheaval would sweep away the Cabinet, including the First Lord, and possibly even the Secretariat—this very man to whom he was talking might be looking for new employment (with a black mark against his name) within a month. It was a tricky situation, and Hornblower suddenly felt overwhelmingly desirous that the interview should be ended. He was horribly hungry and desperately fatigued. When the door opened to admit Dorsey he looked up with relief.

Dorsey halted at sight of Barrow.

"The Secretary is with His Lordship," explained Barrow. "What is it, Mr. Dorsey?"

"I've opened the dispatch that Captain Hornblower captured, sir. It's—it's important, sir."

Dorsey's glance wavered over to Hornblower and back again.

"I think Captain Hornblower is entitled to see the results of his efforts," said Barrow, and Dorsey came forward with relief and laid on the table the objects he was carrying.

First there were half a dozen discs of white wax laid out on a tray.

"I've reproduced the seals," explained Dorsey. "Two copies of each. That seal-cutter in Cheapside can cut a seal from these so that Boney himself couldn't tell the difference. And I've managed to lift the originals without damaging them too much—the hot knife method, you understand, sir."

"Excellent," said Barrow, examining the results. "So these are the seals of the new Empire?"

"Indeed they are, sir. But the dispatch— It's the greatest of prizes. See here, sir! And here!"

He stabbed excitedly at the paper with a gnarled finger. At the foot of the sheet, which was covered with paragraphs of careful handwriting, there was a crabbed signature. It had been written by a careless hand, and was surrounded by little ink blots as a result of the spluttering of a protesting pen. It was not really legible; Hornblower could read the first letters—"Nap . . ."— but the remainder was only a jagged line and a flourish.

"That's the first signature of this sort which has come into our possession, sir," explained Dorsey.

"Do you mean he has always signed 'N. Bonaparte' before?" asked Hornblower.

"Just 'Bonaparte,'" said Dorsey. "We have a hundred, a thousand specimens, but not one like this."

"He hasn't adopted the imperial style, all the same," said Barrow, examining the letter. "Not yet at least. He calls himself 'I' and not 'we.' See here, and here."

"I'm sure you're right, sir," said Dorsey. "But here's something else, sir. And here."

The superscription said *Palais des Tuileries* and *Cabinet Impériale.*

"These are new?" asked Barrow.

"Yes, indeed, sir. Until now he did not call it a palace, and it was the 'Cabinet of the First Consul.'"

"I wonder what the letter says?" interposed Hornblower. So far only the technical details had occupied their attention, like people judging a book by its binding without a thought for its contents. He took it from Dorsey's hand and began to read.

"You read French, sir?" asked Barrow.

"Yes," said Hornblower a little off-handedly, as he concentrated on his reading. He had never read a letter from an emperor before.

The letter was addressed to the general commanding the French Forces in Martinique. *Monsieur le Général Lauriston,* it began. The first paragraph was taken up with allusions to instructions already sent by the Ministries of Marine and of War. The second paragraph dealt with the relative seniority of General Lauriston and of various subordinates. The final one was more flamboyant.

"Hoist my flags over that beautiful continent, and if the British attack you, and you experience some bad luck, always remember three things, activity, concentration of forces, and the firm resolution to die with glory. These are the great principles of war which have brought me success in all my operations. Death is nothing, but to live defeated and without glory is to die every day. Do not worry about your family. Think only about that portion of my family which you are going to reconquer."

"It reads like a counsel of despair, sir," said Hornblower. "Telling him to fight to the last."

"No mention of sending him reinforcements," agreed Barrow. "Quite the opposite, in fact. A pity."

To reinforce the West Indies would necessitate risking some of Bonaparte's naval forces at sea.

"Boney needs a victory here first, sir," suggested Hornblower.

"Yes."

Hornblower found his own bitter smile repeated by Barrow. A victory won by Bonaparte in home waters would mean the conquest of England, the automatic fall of the West Indies and the East Indies, of Canada and the Cape, the whole of England's empire; it would mean an alteration in the destiny of all mankind.

"But this—" said Barrow with a wave of the dispatch. "This may play its part."

Hornblower had already learned the importance of negative information, and he nodded agreement. And it was at that moment that Marsden returned to the room, with a fistful of papers.

"Oh, you're here, Dorsey," he said. "That's for His Majesty at Windsor. See that the courier leaves within fifteen minutes. That's for the telegraph to Plymouth. So's that. That's for Portsmouth. Have the copying begun immediately."

It was interesting to watch Marsden in action; there

was no trace of excitement in his voice, and although the successive sentences followed each other without a pause they did not come tumbling out. Each was clearly enunciated in a tone of apparent indifference. The papers Marsden had brought in might be of vital importance—most certainly they were—but Marsden acted as if he were handing out blank sheets in some meaningless ceremony. His cold eyes passed over Hornblower and fixed on Barrow.

"No further messages, Mr. Barrow?"

"None, Mr. Marsden."

"There will be no confirmation from Plymouth before eight o'clock tomorrow morning," remarked Marsden, looking at the clock.

The telegraph in clear weather and daylight could transmit a message from Plymouth in fifteen minutes—Hornblower had noticed several of the huge semaphore standards during his recent journey; last year he had landed outside Brest and burned a similar machine. But a written message, carried by relays of mounted couriers (some of them riding through darkness) would take twenty-three hours to make the journey. He himself, in his post-chaise, had taken forty; it seemed now as if it were weeks, and not hours.

"This captured dispatch of Captain Hornblower's is of interest, Mr. Marsden," said Barrow; the tone of his voice seemed to echo Marsden's apparent indifference. It was hard for Hornblower to decide whether it was imitation or parody.

It was a matter of moments for Marsden to read the

dispatch and to grasp the importance of the signature.

"So now we might imitate a letter from His Imperial and Royal Majesty the Emperor Napoleon," commented Marsden; the smile that accompanied the words was just as inhuman as the tone of his voice.

Hornblower was experiencing an odd reaction, possibly initiated by this last remark of Marsden's. His head was swimming with hunger and fatigue; he was being projected into a world of unreality, and the unreality was made still more unreal by the manner of these two cold-blooded gentlemen with whom he was closeted. There were stirrings in his brain. Wild—delirious—ideas were forming there, but no wilder than this world in which he found himself, where fleets were set in motion by a word and where an emperor's dispatches could be the subject of a jest. He condemned his notions to himself as lunatic nonsense, and yet even as he did so he found additions making their appearance in his mind, logical contributions building up into a fantastic whole.

Marsden was looking at him—through him—with those cold eyes.

"You may have done a great service for your King and country," said Marsden; the words might be interpreted as words of praise, perhaps, but the manner and expression would require no modification if Marsden were a judge on the bench condemning a criminal.

"I hope I have done so, sir," replied Hornblower.

"Exactly why do you hope that?"

It was a bewildering question, bewildering because its answer was so obvious.

"Because I am a King's officer, sir," said Hornblower.

"And not, Captain, because you expect any reward?"

"I had not thought of it, sir. It was only the purest chance," answered Hornblower.

This was verbal fencing, and faintly irritating. Perhaps Marsden enjoyed the game. Perhaps years of having to throw cold water on the hopes of innumerable ambitious officers demanding promotion and employment had made the process habitual to him.

"A pity it is not a dispatch of real importance," he said. "This only makes clear what we already could guess, that Boney does not intend to send reinforcements to Martinique."

"But with that for a model—" began Hornblower. Then he stopped, angry with himself. His tumultuous thoughts would make still greater nonsense if expressed in words.

"With this as a model?" repeated Marsden.

"Let us have your suggestion, Captain," said Barrow.

"I can't waste your time, gentlemen," stammered Hornblower; he was on the verge of the abyss and striving unavailingly to draw back.

"You have given us an inkling, Captain," said Barrow. "Please continue."

There was nothing else to be done. An end to discretion.

"An order from Boney to Villeneuve, telling him to sail from Ferrol at all costs. It would have to give a reason—say that Decrès has escaped from Brest and will await him at a rendezvous off Cape Clear. So that

97

Villeneuve must sail instantly—weigh, cut, or slip. A battle with Villeneuve is what England needs most—that would bring it about."

Now he had committed himself. Two pairs of eyes were staring at him fixedly.

"An ideal solution, Captain," said Marsden. "If only it could be done. How fine it would be if such an order could be delivered to Villeneuve."

The Secretary to the Board of Admiralty probably received crackpot schemes for the destruction of the French navy every day of the week.

"Boney will be sending orders from Paris, often enough," went on Hornblower. He was not going to give up. "How often do you transmit orders from this office to Commanders in Chief, sir? To Admiral Cornwallis, for instance? Once a week, sir? Oftener?"

"At least," admitted Marsden.

"Boney would write more often that that, I think."

"He would," agreed Barrow.

"And those orders would come by road. Of course Boney would never trust the Spanish postal services. An officer—a French officer, one of the imperial aides-de-camp—would ride with the orders through Spain, from the French frontier to Ferrol."

"Yes?" said Marsden. He was at least interested enough to admit an interrogative note into the monosyllable.

"Captain Hornblower has been engaged in gathering information from the French coast for the last two years," interposed Barrow. "His name was always appearing in Cornwallis's dispatches, Mr. Marsden."

"I know that, Mr. Barrow," said Marsden; there might even be a testy note in his voice at the interruption.

"The dispatch is forged," said Hornblower, taking the final plunge. "A small party is landed secretly with it at a quiet spot on the Spanish Biscay coast, posing as French officials, or Spanish officials, and they travel slowly towards the frontier along the highroad. A succession of couriers approaches from the opposite direction, bearing orders for Villeneuve. Seize one of them, and perhaps with the best of luck substitute the forged order for the one he is carrying. If this cannot be done, kill him—and one of our men, posing as a French officer, turns back and delivers the false letter to Villeneuve."

There was the whole plan, fantastic and yet—and yet—at least faintly possible. At least not demonstrably impossible.

"You say you've seen these Spanish roads, Captain?" asked Barrow.

"I saw something of them, sir."

Hornblower turned back from addressing Barrow to find Marsden's gaze still unwavering, fixed on his face.

"Haven't you any more to say, Captain? Surely you have."

This might be irony; it might be intended to lure him into making a greater and greater fool of himself. But there was so much that was plainly obvious and which he had forborne to mention. His weary mind could still deal with such points, with a moment to put them in order.

"This is an opportunity, gentlemen. A victory at sea is what England needs more than anything else at this moment. Could we measure its value? Could we? It would put an end to Boney's schemes. It would ease the strain of blockade beyond all measure. What would we give for the chance?"

"Millions," said Barrow.

"And what do we risk? Two or three agents. If they fail, that is all we have lost. A penny ticket in a lottery. An infinite gain against an inconsiderable loss."

"You are positively eloquent, Captain," said Marsden, still without any inflexion in his voice.

"I had no intention of being eloquent, sir," said Hornblower, and was a little taken aback at realising how much truth there was in such a simple statement.

He was suddenly annoyed both with himself and with the others. He had allowed himself to be drawn into indiscretions, to appear as one of the feather-brained crackpots for whom Marsden must have so much contempt. He rose in irritation from his chair, and then restrained himself, on the verge of being still more indiscreet by displaying irritation. A stiffly formal attitude would be best; that would indicate that his recent speeches had been mere polite conversation. Moreover, if he were going to preserve any of his self-respect, he must forestall the imminent and inevitable dismissal.

"I have consumed a great deal of your very valuable time, gentlemen," he said.

There was a sudden sharp pleasure, despite his weariness, in thus being the first to make a move, to volunteer to quit the company of the Secretary to the Board, and of the Second Secretary, while dozens of junior officers were prepared to wait hours and days for an interview. But Marsden was addressing Barrow.

"What's the name of that South American fellow who's haunting every ante-room at present, Mr. Barrow? You meet him everywhere—he was even dining at White's last week with Camberwell."

"The fellow who wants to start a revolution, sir? I've met him a couple of times myself. It's—it's Miranda, or Mirandola, something like that, sir."

"Miranda! That's the name. I suppose we can lay hands on him if we want him."

"Easily enough, sir."

"Yes. Now there's Claudius in Newgate Gaol. I understand he was a friend of yours, Mr. Barrow."

"Claudius, sir? I met him, as everyone else did."

"He'll be coming up for trial within the week, I suppose?"

"Yes, sir. He'll swing next Monday. But why are you asking about him, Mr. Marsden?"

Hornblower felt some faint pleasure in seeing the Second Secretary so bewildered; nor was Barrow at the moment being given any satisfaction.

"So there is no time to waste." Marsden turned to Hornblower, who was standing uncomfortably aware that the drama of his exit had fallen a little flat with this delay. "The doorkeeper has your address, Captain?"

"Yes."

"Then I shall send for you very shortly."

"Aye aye, sir."

Hornblower had shut the door before he experienced

any qualm regarding using this purely naval expression towards a civilian, nor did it linger, with so much else for his weary brain to think about. He wanted food; he was desperately in need of sleep. He hardly cared about the unknown Miranda, this mysterious Claudius in Newgate Gaol. What he must do was to eat himself into a torpor, and then sleep, and sleep, and sleep. But also he must write to Maria.

IX

HORNBLOWER awoke in an overheated condition. The sunshine was blazing through the window, and his little attic room was like an oven. Sleep had overcome him while he lay under a blanket, and he was sweating profusely. Throwing off the blanket brought some relief, and he cautiously began to straighten himself out; apparently he had slept without a change of position, literally like a log. There was still an ache or two to be felt, which served to recall to his mind where he was and how he came to be there. His formula for inducing sleep had worked only after a long delay. But it was well after sunrise; he must have slept for ten or perhaps twelve hours.

What day of the week was it? To answer that question called for a plunge into the past. It had been a Sunday that he had spent in the post-chaise—he could remember the church bells sounding across the countryside and the churchgoers gathering round the post-chaise in Salisbury. So that he had arrived in London on Monday morning —yesterday, hard to believe though that was—and today was Tuesday. He had left Plymouth—he had last seen Maria—on Saturday aftenoon. Hornblower felt his pleasant relaxation replaced by tension; he actually felt his muscles tightening ready for action as he went back from there—it was during the small hours of Friday morning that the *Princess* had headed away from the disabled *Guêpe*. It was on Thursday evening that he had climbed onto the deck of the *Guêpe* to conquer or die, with death more probable than conquest. Last Thursday evening, and this was only Tuesday morning.

He tried to put the uncomfortable thoughts away from him; there was a momentary return of tension as an odd thought occurred to him. He had left behind in the Admiralty—he had completely forgotten until now—the French captain's blanket in which he had bundled the ship's papers. Presumably some indigent clerk in the Admiralty had gladly taken it home last night, and there was nothing to be tense about—nothing, provided he did not allow himself to think about the French captain's head shattered like a cracked walnut.

He made himself listen to the street cries outside, and to the rumbling of cart wheels; the diversion allowed him to sink back again into quiescence, into semi-consciousness. It was not until some time later that he drowsily noted the sound of a horse's hoofs outside in the street, a trotting horse, with no accompanying sound of wheels. He raised himself when the clatter stopped under his window. He could guess what it was. But he had progressed no farther than to be standing in his shirt, when steps on the stairs and a thumping on his door checked him.

"Who is it?"

"Admiralty messenger."

Hornblower slid the bolt back in the door. The messenger was there, in blue coat and leather breeches and high boots, under his arm a billycock hat with a black cockade. From behind him peered the stupid face of the landlady's son.

"Captain Hornblower?"

"Yes."

The captain of a ship of war was accustomed to receiving messages in his shirt. Hornblower signed the receipt with the proffered pencil and opened the note.

The Secretary to the Lords Commissioners of the Admiralty would be greatly obliged if Captain Horatio Hornblower would attend at the Admiralty at eleven o'clock A.M. today, Tuesday.

"What's the time now?" asked Hornblower.

"Not long past eight, sir."

"Very well." Hornblower could not resist continuing with a question. "Does the Admiralty send all its messages out on horseback?"

"Only those over a mile, sir." The messenger allowed himself the faintest hint of what he thought of naval officers who lodged on the wrong side of the river.

"Thank you. That will be all."

There was no need for a reply. An affirmative could be taken quite for granted when the Secretary expressed himself as likely to be greatly obliged. Hornblower proceeded to shave and dress.

He took boat across the river, despite the additional

three ha'pence that it cost, first telling himself that he had to go to the post office to hand in his letter to Maria, and then amusedly admitting that it was a temptation to find himself afloat again after three days on land.

"That Calder has let the Frenchies give him the slip, Captain," said the wherryman between leisurely pulls at his sculls.

"We'll know more about it in a day or two," replied Hornblower mildly.

"He caught 'em and let 'em go. Nelson wouldn't 'a done that."

"There's no knowing what Lord Nelson would have done."

"Boney on our doorstep, an' Villain-noove at sea. That Calder! 'E ought to be ashamed. I've 'eard about Admiral Byng an' 'ow they shot 'im. That's what they ought to do with Calder."

That was the first sign Hornblower observed of the storm of indignation roused by the news of the battle off Cape Finisterre. The landlord of the Saracen's Head when Hornblower went in to breakfast was eager with questions, and the two maids stood anxiously listening to the discussion until their mistress sent them about their business.

"Let me see a newspaper," said Hornblower.

"Newspaper, sir? Yes, certainly, sir."

Here was the Gazette Extraordinary, in the place of honour on the front page, but it hardly merited the lofty title, for it consisted of no more than eight lines, and was only a résumé of the first telegraphic dispatch. The full report from Calder, carried up to London by relays of couriers riding ten-mile stages at full speed, would only now be arriving at the Admiralty. It was the editorial comment which was significant, for the *Morning Post* clearly held the same views as the wherryman and the innkeeper. Calder had been stationed to intercept Villeneuve, and the interception had taken place, thanks to good planning by the Admiralty. But Calder had failed in his particular task, which was to destroy Villeneuve once the Admiralty had brought about the meeting.

Villeneuve had arrived from the West Indies, evading Nelson who had followed him there, and had broken through the barrier England had endeavoured to interpose. Now he had reached Ferrol, where he would be able to land his sick, and renew his fresh water, ready to issue forth again to threaten the Channel. Viewed in this light it could be reckoned as a decided French success; Hornblower had no doubt that Bonaparte would represent it as a resounding victory.

"Yes, sir. What do you think, sir?" asked the innkeeper.

"Look out of your door and tell me if Boney's marching down the street," said Hornblower.

It was indicative of the innkeeper's state of mind that he actually made a move towards the door before realisation came to him.

"You are pleased to jest, sir."

There was really nothing to do except to jest. These discussions of naval strategy and tactics by ignorant civilians reminded Hornblower a little of the arguments of the citizens of Gibbon's declining Rome regarding the nature of the Trinity. Yet it was popular clamour that had compelled the death sentence on Byng to be carried out. Calder might be in serious danger of his life.

"The worst thing Boney's done today is to keep me from my breakfast," said Hornblower.

"Yes, sir. Of course, sir. This minute, sir."

It was as the innkeeper bustled away that Hornblower caught sight of another name on the front page of the *Morning Post*. It was a paragraph about Doctor Claudius, and as Hornblower read he remembered why the name had been vaguely familiar to him when Marsden mentioned it. There had been references to him in earlier newspapers, old copies which he had seen even during the blockade of Brest. Claudius was a clergyman, a genuine Doctor of Divinity, and the centre of the most resounding scandal, both social and financial, in English history. He had entered into London society to gain a bishopric for himself, but, while achieving considerable popularity or notoriety, he had failed in his object. Despairing of preferment he had plunged into crime. He had built up an extensive organisation specialising in the forging of bills of exchange. So perfect were his forgeries, and so cunning was his marketing of them, that he had long gone undetected.

The world-wide commerce of England was conducted largely by bills of exchange. Claudius had taken advantage of the long intervals necessary between drawing and presentation to insert his forgeries into the stream, and only an error by a confederate had exposed him. Bills drawn in Beyrout and in Madras, so perfect that the very victims found it hard to dishonour them, were still coming in, and the financial world was shaken to its foundations. Judging by this paragraph, the world of high society which had accepted him was similarly rent. Now Claudius was lodged in Newgate Gaol and his trial was imminent. Was it significant that Marsden had expressed interest in this fellow? Hornblower found it hard to believe it.

At that moment his attention was caught by the sight of his own name in another paragraph. It was headed "Plymouth" and after mentions of the comings and goings of ships came "Captain Horatio Hornblower, late of H.M. Sloop *Hotspur,* landed this morning from the water-hoy *Princess* and immediately took post to London."

It was quite ridiculous that such a triviality should improve the flavour of the gammon and spinach and fried eggs that the innkeeper set before him, but it was indeed the case. It put him in a good humour as he walked towards Whitehall. Marsden must be ready to discuss with him his promotion to captain and to find a ship for him—the sooner this vital business was settled the better. He had no friends in high places now that Cornwallis had hauled down his flag, and Cornwallis's recommendation could easily be shelved or even forgotten in order to make room for a favourite.

It seemed inconceivable to Hornblower, in the clear light of day, after a good night's rest and with a full stomach, that Marsden could have in mind to take any further action on the wild plan to send false orders to Villeneuve. And yet— It was not so inconceivable; nor was it such a wild plan. The forgery would have to be very good, the substitution undetected. As Ferrol was at least ten days by courier from Paris there would be no chance of Villeneuve referring back for confirmation. And because it was inconceivable that the British government should do such a thing, its success, if it were attempted, would be all the more likely.

Here was the Admiralty. This morning he could say with assurance to the doorkeeper, "I have an appointment with Mr. Marsden," to the vast envy of a couple of suppliants who were seeking admission; and he could write "by appointment" on the form on which he stated his business. He was left no more than ten minutes in the waiting room; three minutes after the clock had chimed eleven, he was summoned into Marsden's presence. Barrow was there as well, and Dorsey too, and the sight of them warned Hornblower that the agenda of the meeting might include the inconceivable.

But it was interesting to find that this morning the First Secretary was human enough to spend a little time on preliminaries before plunging into business.

"I'm sure you'll be flattered to hear, Captain, that His Lordship holds practically identical opinions regarding Ferrol as you do."

"I'm very flattered, sir." Lord Barham was not only First Lord, but he had been Comptroller of the Navy for many years and an admiral commanding a fleet before that. He must have been responsible for the orders that had placed Calder across Villeneuve's path.

"His Lordship was both surprised and gratified at Mr. Barrow's familiarity with local conditions there," went on Marsden. "Naturally Mr. Barrow did not see fit to tell him he had just finished discussing them with you."

"Naturally not, sir," agreed Hornblower. Then he braced himself; to speak called for resolution. "Perhaps in that case His Lordship would give favourable consideration to Admiral Cornwallis's recommendation of me to post rank?"

Now it was said. But not a flicker of expression was observable on the faces of the two Secretaries.

"There is more urgent business at present," said Marsden. "We are keeping someone waiting. Dorsey, kindly bring in the parson."

Dorsey walked across and opened the door, and after a moment a short, square figure came waddling in; Hornblower had a glimpse of a uniformed marine outside before the door closed. The newcomer wore a black clerical gown and a clerical wig; but his clerical clothing was at variance with his unshaven cheeks, which bore half an inch of black stubble. His wrists were bound with handcuffs, and a chain ran from the handcuffs to his waist.

"This is the Reverend Doctor Claudius," said Marsden. "Newly arrived from Newgate. His services have been lent to us by the courtesy of the Secretary of State for Home Affairs. Temporarily, at least."

Claudius looked round at them all with an expression

which offered an interesting study in psychology. He had bold black eyes, yet they were cunning and sly. There was fear in his pudgy face, yet there was defiance as well; most interesting of all, there was curiosity, irrepressible even in the shadow of death.

Marsden wasted no time. "Claudius, you've been brought here to execute a forgery, if you can."

The pudgy face showed a sudden flash of understanding, and then instantly settled into an immobility which called forth Hornblower's admiration.

"Both politeness and convention," said Claudius, "suggest that you address me as 'Doctor.' I have not yet been unfrocked, and I am still a Doctor of Divinity."

"Rubbish, Claudius," said Marsden.

"I shouldn't have expected politeness from underlings!"

Claudius' voice was an unpleasant one, harsh and grating, which might explain the ill success of his quest for a bishopric. Nevertheless, Claudius had taken the offensive in this first exchange—that letter from Bonaparte which Dorsey held had recommended an unexpected counter-attack vigorously carried out even with an inferior force.

But the Admiralty's campaign was commanded by a master of tactics. "Very well, Doctor," said Marsden. "The dignity of a Doctor of Divinity demands all the respect we can accord it. Mr. Dorsey, hand that document to the Doctor with the compliments of Their Lordships of the Admiralty, and ask the Doctor if, as a result of his vast experience, he thinks himself capable of making anything similar."

Claudius took the thing in his manacled hands, and his black eyebrows came together as he studied it.

"Of French origin. That is plain. Apart from the language it is in the standard handwriting in use by French clerks. I had plenty of examples pass through my hands during the late peace."

"And the signature?"

"An interesting piece of work. Written with a turkey quill, I should say. It would call for at least an hour's practice before I could reproduce it. Now these seals—"

"I made moulds," said Dorsey.

"I could see that. But they have been lifted from the paper with reasonable care. I must congratulate you on your acquirement of a difficult art. Now—"

Claudius looked up from the paper and swept his audience with a searching glance.

"Gentlemen," he said, "I have much more to say on this subject. But before I do so, I need some assurance that my services will not go without recompense."

"You are having that already," said Marsden. "Your trial has been postponed for a week."

"A week? I used to preach sermons on how speedily time passes from Sunday to Sunday. No, gentlemen. I need my life. I have a mortal objection to hanging, and that is not spoken in jest."

The situation was tense with drama. Hornblower looked round at the four faces—Marsden displaying the faintest possible hint of cynical amusement, Barrow a little taken aback, Dorsey displaying the proper indifference of a subordinate, and Claudius looking warily from one to another, like a condemned criminal in the Roman arena watching the lions close in on him. Barrow spoke first, addressing Marsden.

"I'll call in the guard, sir, shall I? We don't need him."

There was yet no slackening in the tension.

"Call in the guard!" said Claudius; there was a clank of iron as he waved his manacled hands. "Take me away, and hang me tomorrow! Tomorrow? A week hence? If it is coming, the sooner the better. You gentlemen may never know the truth of that statement. I still have charity enough to hope that you never will. But true it is. Hang me tomorrow."

Hornblower found it hard to decide whether Claudius was gambling or not, staking a week of life which might well be dear to him against the possibility of pardon. But he could not help feeling a guilty twinge of admiration for the ugly little man, alone and helpless, fighting his last battle and refusing to lapse into a mere plea for mercy—especially when that, addressed to Marsden, would have been the least effective plea of all. Then Marsden spoke.

"You will not hang," he said.

Ever since Claudius had been brought in the sky had been darkening. After a few days of sunny summer weather the inevitable thunderstorm of the Thames valley was building up, and there was a low rumble of thunder following Marsden's words. Hornblower was reminded of the thunder in the *Iliad* which confirmed the oath taken by Zeus.

Claudius darted a piercing glance at Marsden.

"Then we are agreed and I shall give you all the benefit of my experience," he said.

Hornblower felt another spurt of admiration; the little man had been content with the four simple words spoken by Marsden. He had not gone through any ceremony of exacting a formal promise; as a gentleman he had instantly accepted a gentleman's word. He may even have been encouraged by the peal of confirmatory thunder.

"Very well," said Marsden, and Claudius plunged into his subject. Only a slight gulping and hesitation as he began betrayed the agonising strain he had been under.

"It is necessary first," he said, "to point out that ambition may outreach itself. It is quite impossible to forge a long document in the handwriting of another and to achieve deception. I take it you have in mind a letter and not a mere few words? Then it would be better to make no attempt at exact reproduction. On the other hand carelessness would easily be fatal. This script, as I said, is the standard script used by French clerks—I fancy it is the one which used to be taught in Jesuit schools. There are French refugees in plenty. Have one of them write your letter."

"That's very true, sir," said Dorsey to Marsden.

"And again," went on Claudius, "have your letter

composed by a Frenchman. You gentlemen may pride yourselves on writing good French, grammatical French, but a Frenchman reading it would know it was not written by a Frenchman. I'll go further than that, gentlemen. Give a Frenchman a passage in English and tell him to render it into French and a Frenchman will *still* be aware that all is not well when he reads it. You must have your French composed ab initio by a Frenchman, contenting yourselves with merely outlining what is to be said."

Hornblower caught Marsden nodding agreement. It was apparent that he was impressed, however little he wished to appear so.

"Now, gentlemen," went on Claudius. "With regard to details of a lower degree of sensibility. I take it you have in mind to send your forged letter to a naval, or possibly a military, man? In that case the task can be approached with more confidence. Business men, soulless bankers, hardheaded merchants—men with something more important to lose than other men's lives—are likely to scrutinise documents very closely. But there is still the risk that some interfering underling on the staff of a general may wish to call attention to himself. It is necessary to be quite perfect. This signature I am confident I can reproduce in perfection. This ink—I believe it can be matched in Chancery Lane; it will be necessary to make complete tests. This printed heading—you will need to have type specially cast in exact imitation. You will have less trouble in that respect than I encountered."

"Yes," said Marsden, actually betrayed into speech.

"But the paper—" went on Claudius, feeling its texture carefully with stubby but apparently sensitive fingers. "I will have to instruct you where to search for that, too. Would you be so kind, sir, as to hold the sheet up between my eyes and the light? This chain restricts my movements to an inconvenient degree. Thank you, sir. Yes, as I thought. I know that quality of linen, but there is a fortunate absence of watermark. It may not be necessary to have paper made de novo to match it. You may not appreciate the necessity for uniformity, gentlemen, unless you make use of your imagination. A single document may well be accepted, but you must think of a series. After receiving, let us say, six genuine documents, someone receives one spurious one. The recipient naturally lays them together in the course of the routine of his office. If one is markedly different from all the others—even if one is different in only a small degree—attention is clamorously called to it. Hinc illae lachrymae. And if that one document has a content somewhat unusual—even though in other circumstances it might have passed—then the fat is in the fire, and Bow Street is called in. Et ego in arcadia vixi, gentlemen."

"Most illuminating," said Marsden, and Hornblower knew enough about him now to realise that this was the equivalent of a long speech in praise.

"Now I come to 'lastly' in my present sermon, gentlemen," said Claudius, as the lightning flashed again and the thunder rolled. "Even in the pulpit I could feel the relief in my congregation at that word 'lastly,' so I will be brief. The method of delivery must conform to the method of all the other deliveries. Once again, the greatest care is necessary in allowing nothing to call particular attention to this one item out of all the others."

Claudius when he had entered the room had been of a sickly pallor under the bristling beard, and he was whiter still when he finished his lecture.

"Perhaps, gentlemen, you would permit me to sit down?" he said. "I have not now the strength of which I used once to boast."

"Take him out, Dorsey," snapped Marsden. "Give him a glass of wine. I dare say he's hungry, too."

It may have been at the thought of food that Claudius recovered something of his unabashed self-assertion.

"A beefsteak, gentlemen?" he said. "Might I hope for a beefsteak? For the past week, empty dreams of a beefsteak have further embittered my nightmares of the rope."

"See that he has a beefsteak, Dorsey," said Marsden.

At the door, Claudius turned back, something of a smile just visible on his stubbled face.

"In that case, gentlemen, you can count on my heartiest exertions for my King, my country, and myself."

With the departure of Dorsey and Claudius, Marsden turned to face Hornblower again. The room was almost dark, at high noon, with the black thunderclouds low overhead. A sudden lightning flash filled the room, instantly followed by a clap of thunder—a vast cannon shot, coming without warning and ending without reverberation.

"His Lordship," said Marsden, still imperturbable, "has already approved in principle of the attempt being made. I consulted him this morning. Mr. Barrow, I am sure, has in mind the French émigrés to attend to the composition and writing of the dispatch."

"I have, Mr. Marsden," said Barrow.

"It will be necessary to recapture the style, of course, sir," said Hornblower.

"Undoubtedly, Captain," agreed Barrow.

"And the orders must be such that there is nothing patently impossible about them, too."

Marsden intervened.

"Did your grandmother never learn to suck eggs, Captain?" he asked, in the same unvarying tone. It was a deft reminder that the Secretaries had had years of experience in the writing of orders, and Hornblower had the sense to smile.

"I had forgotten how much practice she has had," he said. "I beg your pardon, gentlemen. I was only anxious about the success of the plan."

Now the thunderstorm had burst. A breath of cooler air came stealing into the room, bearing with it the sound of torrential rain roaring down outside. Through the windows there was nothing to be seen but the rain.

"Mr. Barrow and Dorsey and Claudius can be trusted to deal with the details. The next point to consider is the landing."

"That should be the simplest part of the whole operation, sir."

The Spanish Biscay coast, sparsely populated and rugged, extended for almost three hundred miles from the French frontier to Ferrol. There were inlets innumerable. The Royal Navy, omnipresent at sea, could be relied upon to put a small party on shore undetected.

"I am delighted that you think so, Captain," said Marsden.

There was a dramatic pause—a melodramatic pause. Hornblower looked from Marsden to Barrow and back again, and experienced an internal upheaval as he observed the glances they exchanged.

"What have you in mind, gentlemen?" he asked.

"Is it not quite obvious, Captain, that you are the man best fitted to undertake this mission?"

That was what Marsden said, in that same tone. Barrow spoke in his support.

"You are acquainted with Ferrol, Captain. You have had some experience of Spain. You speak a little Spanish. You should have command."

That gave the cue for Marsden again.

"You have no other command at present, Captain."

The significance of this particular remark was too obvious. "Really, gentlemen—" said Hornblower. For once he could not think quickly enough to word his protests.

"It is not a duty you could be ordered to perform," went on Marsden. "That is quite clear. It would be a purely voluntary mission."

To enter a hostile country in disguise would be to risk a shameful death. The gallows, the rope—but in Spain it would be the iron collar of the garotte. Strangulation. Convulsions, contortions, preceding death. No fighting service could ever order its officers to take that risk.

"This Spaniard, Miranda, can be trusted, I am sure," said Barrow. "And if a Frenchman is needed as well—your opinion on that point would be valuable, Captain—there are at least three who have already done important work for us."

It was inconceivable that these two Secretaries, men of marble, could ever abase themselves to plead, but it seemed as if they were as close to doing so as ever in their lives. The Navy could order a man to climb the highest, steepest side of a ship of the line in the face of well-aimed musketry; it took for granted that a man would face, unflinching, broadside after broadside of grape; it could send him aloft on the darkest and stormiest night to save a few yards of canvas; and it could hang him or shoot him or flog him to death should he hesitate. But it could not order him to risk the garotte, not even with the nation's existence trembling in the balance.

It was this—this recollection of England's desperate need—that overshadowed every other consideration. In the calm atmosphere of this very room Hornblower had pleaded the vital need for a victory at sea, and had balanced against it the trifling cost of his suggested plan. That cost might be his own life, it now appeared. But—but—whom could he trust to keep a clear head, whom could he trust to plan and to extemporise in an emergency? Already, unsought, there were forming in his mind improvements, refinements, in the rough plan which demanded his own personal action. He would have to agree; and in a moment of illumination he felt that he would never be happy again if he were to refuse. He must say yes.

"Captain," said Marsden. "We have not forgotten Admiral Cornwallis's recommendation that you should be made post."

The speech was so utterly disassociated from Hornblower's present train of thought, so unrelated to what he had been about to say, that he found he could not speak. Barrow glanced over at Marsden and then made his contribution.

"There would be no need to find you a ship, Captain," he said. "You could be given a command in the Sea Fencibles which would confer post rank. Then you could be transferred for special service."

Indeed this was something alien intruding into the conversation. This was what Hornblower had given more than a passing thought to on his way here. Promotion to captain's rank! He would be "made post," placed on the list of captains. He would cease to be a mere commander addressed as "captain" only by convention. He would be a real captain, he would have achieved the ambition of every naval officer down to the lowest King's letterboy in the service; once on the list only a court martial or death could stop his eventually becoming an admiral.

And he had quite forgotten about promotion; he had forgotten his decision to press for it. It was not so surprising that he had forgotten about the Sea Fencibles—they constituted a volunteer reserve navy formed of wherrymen and bargees and fishermen who could be called into active service should an actual attempt at invasion occur. England was divided into districts for the organisation and elementary training of these men, and each district was a captain's command—a post captain's command.

"Well, Captain?" asked Marsden.

"I'll do it," said Hornblower.

He saw glances interchanged again; he could see relief, or perhaps satisfaction, or perhaps self-congratulation in those glances. The Secretaries were pleased that their bribe had been effective, and he was about to burst out in an indignant denial that the offer had had any weight with him. Then he shut his mouth again, remembering the philosopher who said that he had often regretted having spoken but had never regretted remaining silent. A few seconds of silence—utterly fortuitous—had won him promotion to post rank; a few seconds of speech might imperil it. And he knew, too, that those two cynical men would not believe any such protestations for a moment. His apparent bargaining might even have won their respect; certainly they would deem a denial to be hypocritical and worthy of contempt.

"Then I had better arrange for you to make Miranda's acquaintance, Captain," said Marsden. "And I should be obliged if you would consider and elaborate a detailed plan for me to submit to His Lordship."

"Yes, sir."

"Orally, if you please. Nothing may be committed to paper regarding this plan, Captain. Except possibly your final report after achieving success."

"I understand, sir."

Was there the slightest hint of softening in Marsden's expression? That last sentence of his was undoubtedly meant as a joke; it was something entirely out of the ordinary. Hornblower had a sudden insight; the Secretary, in addition to all his routine work, carried a responsibility which must occasion him considerable anxiety. Transient First Lords and Sea Lords could not maintain the needed continuity, and the First Secretary had necessarily to deal with all matters of this sort, the gathering of information, the dissemination of false information —with spying, in fact, to use a single and ugly word. Hornblower could see already now how difficult it must be to find reliable agents, men who could be trusted not to play a double role. Marsden was experiencing relief at this moment, to such an extent that he actually allowed it to show.

"I will make the arrangements for your posting to be gazetted, Captain." This was Barrow, attending to details. "You will read yourself in before the end of the week."

"Very well, sir."

When Hornblower reached the street the rain was falling more softly, although with every appearance of continuing for a long time. He had no cloak, no tarpaulin, but he went out into the rain quite gladly. He felt he must walk and walk and walk. The rain on his face was pleasant, and he told himself that the soft rainwater would dissolve out the clammy sea-salt with which all his clothes were impregnated. The thought only distracted him for a moment from the others that were writhing in his brain like eels in a sack. He was about to become a captain at last, and he was about to become a spy.

From the Author's Notes

Hornblower goes through a period of training in prepara-
tion for his spy mission. He brushes up his Spanish with the
ruddy-complexioned Count Miranda; he is to accompany the
Count to Spain disguised as his servant. "He would have to
watch every word and gesture; his life depended on doing
nothing that would betray them." Then Hornblower goes
through a crisis of conscience about becoming a spy.

As he is rowed towards the ship that will take him from
Spithead to Spain, Hornblower thinks: One stage further
along a hateful voyage. Each stroke of the boatmen's oars is
carrying him nearer to a time of frightful strain; to something
close to a certainty of shameful and hideous death . . .

He wonders whether to turn back, but sense of duty pre-
vails. A forged letter is delivered to Villeneuve, which prompts
the French to come out and fight.

This is what Hornblower wants. It leads to the victory at
Trafalgar. The course of history is changed.

Hornblower's Temptation

THE Channel Fleet was taking shelter at last. The roaring westerly gales had worked up to such a pitch that timber and canvas and cordage could withstand them no longer, and nineteen ships of the line and seven frigates, with Admiral Lord Bridport flying his flag in H.M.S. *Victory,* had momentarily abandoned that watch over Brest which they had maintained for six years. Now they were rounding Berry Head and dropping anchor in the shelter of Tor Bay. A landsman, with that wind shrieking round him, might be pardoned for wondering how much shelter was to be found there, but to the weary and weather-beaten crews who had spent so long tossing in the Biscay waves and clawing away from the rocky coast of Brittany, that foam-whitened anchorage was like paradise. Boats could even be sent in to Brixham and Torquay to return with letters and fresh water; in most of the ships, officers and men had gone for three months without either. Even on that winter day there was intense physical pleasure in opening the throat and pouring down it a draught of fresh clear water, so different from the stinking green liquid doled out under guard yesterday.

The junior lieutenant in H.M.S. *Renown* was walking the deck muffled in his heavy pea-jacket while his ship wallowed at her anchor. The piercing wind set his eyes watering, but he continually gazed through his telescope nevertheless; for, as signal lieutenant, he was responsible for the rapid reading and transmission of messages, and this was a likely moment for orders to be given regarding sick and stores, and for captains and admirals to start chattering together, for invitations to dinner to be passed back and forth, and even for news to be disseminated.

He watched a small boat claw its way toward the ship from the French prize the fleet had snapped up yesterday on its way up-Channel. Hart, master's mate, had been sent on board from the *Renown,* as prizemaster, miraculously making the perilous journey. Now here was Hart, with the prize safely anchored amid the fleet, returning on board to make some sort of report. That hardly seemed likely to be of interest to a signal lieutenant, but Hart appeared excited as he came on board, and hurried below with his news after reporting himself in the briefest terms to the officer of the watch. But only a very few minutes passed before the signal lieutenant found himself called upon to be most active.

It was Captain Sawyer himself who came on deck, Hart following him, to supervise the transmission of the messages. "Mr. Hornblower!"

"Sir!"

"Kindly send this signal."

It was for the admiral himself, from the captain; that

part was easy; only two hoists were necessary to say *"Renown* to Flag." And there were other technical terms which could be quickly expressed—"prize" and "French" and "brig"—but there were names which would have to be spelled out letter for letter. "Prize is French national brig *Espérance* having on board Barry McCool."

"Mr. James!" bellowed Hornblower. The signal midshipman was waiting at his elbow, but midshipmen should always be bellowed at, especially by a lieutenant with a very new commission.

Hornblower reeled off the numbers, and the signal went soaring up to the yard-arm; the signal halliards vibrated wildly as the gale tore at the flags. Captain Sawyer waited on deck for the reply; this business must be important. Hornblower read the message again, for until that moment he had only studied it as something to be transmitted. But even on re-reading it he did not know why the message should be important. Until three months before, he had been a prisoner in Spanish hands for two weary years, and there were gaps in his knowledge of recent history. The name of Barry McCool meant nothing to him.

On the other hand, it seemed to mean a great deal to the admiral, for hardly had sufficient time elapsed for the message to be carried below to him than a question soared up to the *Victory's* yard-arm.

"Flag to *Renown,*" Hornblower read those flags as they broke and was instantly ready for the rest of the message. "Is McCool alive?"

"Reply affirmative," said Captain Sawyer.

And the affirmative had hardly been hoisted before the next signal was fluttering in the *Victory*.

"Have him on board at once. Court-martial will assemble."

A court-martial! Who on earth was this man McCool? A deserter? The recapture of a mere deserter would not be a matter for the commander in chief. A traitor? Strange that a traitor should be court-martialled in the fleet. But there it was. A word from the captain sent Hart scurrying overside to bring this mysterious prisoner on board, while signal after signal went up from the *Victory* convening the court-martial in the *Renown*.

Hornblower was kept busy enough reading the messages; he had only a glance to spare when Hart had his prisoner and his sea-chest hoisted up over the port side. A youngish man, tall and slender, his hands were tied behind him—which was why he had to be hoisted in—and he was hatless, so that his long red hair streamed in the wind. He wore a blue uniform with red facings—a French infantry uniform, apparently. The name, the uniform and the red hair combined to give Hornblower his first insight into the situation. McCool must be an Irishman. While Hornblower had been a prisoner in Ferrol, there had been, he knew, a bloody rebellion in Ireland. Irishmen who had escaped had taken service with France in large number. This must be one of them, but it hardly explained why the admiral should take it upon himself to try him instead of handing him over to the civil authorities.

Hornblower had to wait an hour for the explanation,

until, at two bells in the next watch, dinner was served in the gunroom.

"There'll be a pretty little ceremony tomorrow morning," said Clive, the surgeon. He put his hand to his neck in a gesture which Hornblower thought hideous.

"I hope the effect will be salutary," said Roberts, the second lieutenant. The foot of the table, where he sat, was for the moment the head, because Buckland, the first lieutenant, was absent attending to the preparations for the court-martial.

"But why should we hang him?" asked Hornblower. Roberts rolled an eye on him.

"Deserter," he said, and then went on. "Of course, you're a newcomer. I entered him myself, into this very ship, in '98. Hart spotted him at once."

"But I thought he was a rebel?"

"A rebel as well," said Roberts. "The quickest way out of Ireland—the only way, in fact—in '98 was to join the armed forces."

"I see," said Hornblower.

"We got a hundred hands that autumn," said Smith, another lieutenant.

And no questions would be asked, thought Hornblower. His country, fighting for her life, needed seamen as a drowning man needs air, and was prepared to make them out of any raw material that presented itself.

"McCool deserted one dark night when we were becalmed off the Penmarks," explained Roberts. "Got through a lower gunport with a grating to float him. We thought he was drowned until news came through from

Paris that he was there, up to his old games. He boasted of what he'd done—that's how we knew him to be O'Shaughnessy, as he called himself when we had him."

"Wolfe Tone had a French uniform," said Smith. "And they'd have strung him up if he hadn't cut his own throat first."

"Uniform only aggravates the offense when he's a deserter," said Roberts.

Hornblower had much to think about. First there was the nauseating thought that there would be an execution in the morning. Then there was this eternal Irish problem, about which the more he thought the more muddled he became. If just the bare facts were considered, there could be no problem. In the world at the moment, Ireland could choose only between the domination of England and the domination of France; no other possibility existed in a world at war. And it seemed unbelievable that anyone would wish to escape from English overlordship—absentee landlords and Catholic disabilities notwithstanding—in order to submit to the rapacity and cruelty and venality of the French republic. To risk one's life to effect such an exchange would be a most illogical thing to do, but logic, Hornblower concluded sadly, had no bearing upon patriotism, and the bare facts were the least considerable factors.

And in the same way the English methods were subject to criticism as well. There could be no doubt that the Irish people looked upon Wolfe Tone and Fitzgerald as martyrs, and would look upon McCool in the same light.

There was nothing so effective as a few martyrdoms to ennoble and invigorate a cause.

The hanging of McCool would merely be adding fuel to the fire that England sought to extinguish. Two peoples actuated by the most urgent of motives—self-preservation and patriotism—were at grips in a struggle which could have no satisfactory ending for any lengthy time to come.

Buckland, the first lieutenant, came into the gunroom with the preoccupied look commonly worn by first lieutenants with a weight of responsibility on their shoulders. He ran his glance over the assembled company, and all the junior officers, sensing that unpleasant duties were about to be allocated, did their unobtrusive best not to meet his eye. Inevitably it was the name of the most junior lieutenant which rose to Buckland's lips.

"Mr. Hornblower," he said.

"Sir!" replied Hornblower, doing his best now to keep resignation out of his voice.

"I am going to make you responsible for the prisoner."

"Sir?" said Hornblower, with a different intonation.

"Hart will be giving evidence at the court-martial," explained Buckland—it was a vast condescension that he should deign to explain at all. "The master-at-arms is a fool, as you know. I want McCool brought up for trial safe and sound, and I want him kept safe and sound afterward. I'm repeating the captain's own words, Mr. Hornblower."

"Aye aye, sir," said Hornblower, for there was nothing else to be said.

"No Wolfe Tone tricks with McCool," said Smith.

Wolfe Tone had cut his own throat the night before he was due to be hanged, and had died in agony a week later.

"Ask me for anything you may need, Mr. Hornblower," said Buckland.

"Aye aye, sir."

"Sideboys!" suddenly roared a voice on deck overhead, and Buckland hurried out; the approach of an officer of rank meant that the court-martial was beginning to assemble.

Hornblower's chin was on his breast. It was a hard, unrelenting world, and he was an officer in the hardest and most unrelenting service in that world—a service in which a man could no more say "I cannot" than he could say "I dare not."

"Bad luck, Horny," said Smith, with surprising gentleness, and there were other murmurs of sympathy from round the table.

"Obey orders, young man," said Roberts quietly.

Hornblower rose from his chair. He could not trust himself to speak, so that it was with a hurried bow that he quitted the company at the table.

" 'E's 'ere, safe an' sound, Mr. 'Ornblower," said the master-at-arms, halting in the darkness of the lower 'tween-decks.

A marine sentry at the door moved out of the way, and the master-at-arms shone the light of his candle-lantern on a keyhole in the door and inserted the key.

"I put 'im in this empty storeroom, sir," went on the master-at-arms. " 'E's got two of my corporals along with 'im."

The door opened, revealing the light of another candle-lantern. The air inside the room was foul; McCool was sitting on a chest, while two of the ship's corporals sat on the deck with their backs to the bulkhead. The corporals rose at an officer's entrance, but even so, there was almost no room for the two newcomers. Hornblower cast a vigilant eye round the arrangements. There appeared to be no chance of escape or suicide. In the end, he steeled himself to meet McCool's eyes.

"I have been put in charge of you," he said.

"That is most gratifying to me, Mr.—Mr.—" said McCool, rising from the chest.

"Hornblower."

"I am delighted to make your acquaintance, Mr. Hornblower."

McCool spoke in a cultured voice, with only enough of Ireland in it to betray his origin. He had tied back the red locks into a neat queue, and even in the faint candle-light his blue eyes gave strange reflections.

"Is there anything you need?" asked Hornblower.

"I could eat and I could drink," replied McCool. "Seeing that nothing has passed my lips since the *Espérance* was captured."

That was yesterday. The man had had neither food nor water for more than twenty-four hours.

"I will see to it," said Hornblower. "Anything more?"

"A mattress—a cushion—something on which I can sit," said McCool. He waved a hand toward his sea-chest. "I bear an honoured name, but I have no desire to bear it imprinted on my person."

The sea-chest was of a rich mahogany. The lid was a thick slab of wood whose surface had been chiselled down to leave his name—B. I. McCool—standing out in high relief.

"I'll send you in a mattress too," said Hornblower.

A lieutenant in uniform appeared at the door.

"I'm Payne, on the admiral's staff," he explained to Hornblower. "I have orders to search this man."

"Certainly," said Hornblower.

"You have my permission," said McCool.

The master-at-arms and his assistants had to quit the crowded little room to enable Payne to do his work, while Hornblower stood in the corner and watched. Payne was quick and efficient. He made McCool strip to the skin and examined his clothes with care—seams, linings and buttons. He crumpled each portion carefully, with his ear to the material, apparently to hear if there were papers concealed inside. Then he knelt down to the chest; the key was already in the lock, and he swung it open. Uniforms, shirts, underclothing, gloves; each article was taken out, examined and laid aside. There were two small portraits of children, to which Payne gave special attention without discovering anything.

"The things you are looking for," said McCool, "were all dropped overside before the prize crew could reach the *Espérance*. You'll find nothing to betray my fellow countrymen, and you may as well save yourself that trouble."

"You can put your clothes on again," said Payne curtly to McCool. He nodded to Hornblower and hurried out again.

"A man whose politeness is quite overwhelming," said McCool, buttoning his breeches.

"I'll attend to your requests," said Hornblower.

He paused only long enough to enjoin the strictest vigilance on the master-at-arms and the ship's corporals before hastening away to give orders for McCool to be given food and water, and he returned quickly. McCool drank his quart of water eagerly, and made an effort to eat the ship's biscuit and meat.

"No knife. No fork," he commented.

"No," replied Hornblower in a tone devoid of expression.

"I understand."

It was strange to stand there gazing down at this man who was going to die tomorrow, biting not very efficiently at the lump of tough meat which he held to his teeth.

The bulkhead against which Hornblower leaned vibrated slightly, and the sound of a gun came faintly down to them. It was the signal that the court-martial was about to open.

"Do we go?" asked McCool.

"Yes."

"Then I can leave this delicious food without any breach of good manners."

Up the ladders to the maindeck, two marines leading, McCool following them, Hornblower following him, and the two ship's corporals bringing up the rear.

"I have frequently traversed these decks," said McCool, looking round him, "with less ceremonial."

Hornblower was watching carefully lest he should break away and throw himself into the sea.

The court-martial. Gold lace and curt efficient routine, as the *Renown* swung to her anchors and the timbers of the ship transmitted the sound of the rigging vibrating in the gale. Evidence of identification. Curt questions.

"Nothing I could say would be listened to amid these emblems of tyranny," said McCool in reply to the president of the court.

It needed no more than fifteen minutes to condemn a man to death: "The sentence of this court is that you, Barry Ignatius McCool, be hanged by the neck—"

The storeroom to which Hornblower escorted McCool back was now a condemned cell. A hurrying midshipman asked for Hornblower almost as soon as they arrived there.

"Captain's compliments, sir, and he'd like to speak to you."

"Very good," said Hornblower.

"The admiral's with him, sir," added the midshipman in a burst of confidence.

Rear Admiral the Honorable Sir William Cornwallis was indeed in the captain's cabin, along with Payne and

Captain Sawyer. He started to go straight to the point the moment Hornblower had been presented to him.

"You're the officer charged with carrying out the execution?" he asked.

"Yes, sir."

"Now look'ee here, young sir—"

Cornwallis was a popular admiral, strict but kindly, and of unflinching courage and towering professional ability. Under his nickname of "Billy Blue" he was the hero of uncounted anecdotes and ballads. But having got so far in what he was intending to say, he betrayed a hesitation alien to his character. Hornblower waited for him to continue.

"Look'ee here," said Cornwallis again. "There's to be no speechifying when he's strung up."

"No, sir?" said Hornblower.

"A quarter of the hands in this ship are Irish," went on Cornwallis. "I'd as lief have a light taken into the magazine as have McCool make a speech to 'em."

"I understand, sir," said Hornblower.

But there was a ghastly routine about executions. From time immemorial the condemned man had been allowed to address his last words to the onlookers.

"String him up," said Cornwallis, "and that'll show 'em what to expect if they run off. But once let him open his mouth— That fellow has the gift of the gab, and we'll have this crew unsettled for the next six months."

"Yes, sir."

"So see to it, young sir. Fill him full o' rum, maybe. But let him speak at your peril."

"Aye aye, sir."

Payne followed Hornblower out of the cabin when he was dismissed.

"You might stuff his mouth with oakum," he suggested. "With his hands tied he could not get it out."

"Yes," said Hornblower, his blood running cold.

"I've found a priest for him," went on Payne, "but he's Irish too. We can't rely on him to tell McCool to keep his mouth shut."

"Yes," said Hornblower.

"McCool's devilish cunning. No doubt he'd throw everything overboard before they captured him."

"What was he intending to do?" asked Hornblower.

"Land in Ireland and stir up fresh trouble. Lucky we caught him. Lucky, for that matter, we could charge him with desertion and make a quick business of it."

"Yes," said Hornblower.

"Don't rely on making him drunk," said Payne, "although that was Billy Blue's advice. Drunk or sober, these Irishmen can always talk. I've given you the best hint."

"Yes," said Hornblower, concealing a shudder.

He went back into the condemned cell like a man condemned himself. McCool was sitting on the straw mattress Hornblower had had sent in, and the two ship's corporals still had him under their observation.

"Here comes Jack Ketch," said McCool with a smile that almost escaped appearing forced.

Hornblower plunged into the matter in hand; he could see no tactful way of approach.

"Tomorrow—" he said.

"Yes, tomorrow?"

"Tomorrow you are to make no speeches," he said.

"None? No farewell to my countrymen?"

"No."

"You are robbing a condemned man of his last privilege."

"I have my orders," said Hornblower.

"And you propose to enforce them?"

"Yes."

"May I ask how?"

"I can stop your mouth with tow," said Hornblower brutally.

McCool looked at the pale, strained face. "You do not appear to me to be the ideal executioner," said McCool, and then a new idea seemed to strike him. "Supposing I were to save you that trouble?"

"How?"

"I could give you my parole to say nothing."

Hornblower tried to conceal his doubts as to whether he could trust a fanatic about to die.

"Oh, you wouldn't have to trust my bare word," said McCool bitterly. "We can strike a bargain, if you will. You need not carry out your half unless I have already carried out mine."

"A bargain?"

"Yes. Allow me to write to my widow. Promise me to send her the letter and my sea-chest here—you can see it is of sentimental value—and I, on my side, promise to say no word from the time of leaving this place here until

—until—" Even McCool faltered at that point. "Is that explicit enough?"

"Well—" said Hornblower.

"You can read the letter," added McCool. "You saw that other gentleman search my chest. Even though you send these things to Dublin, you can be sure that they contain nothing of what you would call treason."

"I'll read the letter before I agree," said Hornblower.

It seemed a way out of a horrible situation. There would be small trouble about finding a coaster destined for Dublin; for a few shillings he could send letter and chest there.

"I'll send you in pen and ink and paper," said Hornblower.

It was time to make the other hideous preparations. To have a whip rove at the port-side fore yard-arm, and to see that the line ran easily through the block. To weight the line and mark a ring with chalk on the gangway where the end rested. To see that the noose ran smooth. To arrange with Buckland for ten men to be detailed to pull when the time came. Hornblower went through it all like a man in a nightmare.

Back in the condemned cell, McCool was pale and wakeful, but he could still force a smile.

"You can see that I had trouble wooing the muse," he said.

At his feet lay a couple of sheets of paper, and Hornblower, glancing at them, could see that they were covered with what looked like attempts at writing poetry. The erasures and alterations were numerous.

146

"But here is my fair copy," said McCool, handing over another sheet.

"My darling wife," the letter began. "It is hard to find words to say farewell to my very dearest—"

It was not easy for Hornblower to force himself to read that letter. It was as if he had to peer through a mist to make out the words. But they were only the words of a man writing to his beloved, whom he would never see again. That at least was plain. He compelled himself to read through the affectionate sentences. At the end it said: "I append a poor poem by which in the years to come you may remember me, my dearest love. And now good-bye, until we shall be together in heaven. Your husband, faithful unto death, Barry Ignatius McCool."

Then came the poem.

Ye heavenly powers! Stand by me when I die!
The bee ascends before my rolling eye.
Life still goes on within the heartless town.
Dark forces claim my soul. So strike 'em down.
The sea will rise, the sea will fall. So turn
Full circle. Turn again. And then will burn
The lambent flames while hell will lift its head.
So pray for me while I am numbered with the dead.

Hornblower read through the turgid lines and puzzled over their obscure imagery. But he wondered if he would be able to write a single line that would make sense if he knew he was going to die in a few hours.

"The superscription is on the other side," said McCool,

and Hornblower turned the sheet over. The letter was addressed to the Widow McCool, in some street in Dublin.

"Will you accept my word now?" asked McCool.

"Yes," said Hornblower.

The horrible thing was done in the grey hours of the morning.

"Hands to witness punishment."

The pipes twittered and the hands assembled in the waist, facing forward. The marines stood in lines across the deck. There were masses and masses of white faces, which Hornblower saw when he brought McCool up from below. There was a murmur when McCool appeared. Around the ship lay boats from all the rest of the fleet, filled with men—men sent to witness the punishment, but ready also to storm the ship should the crew stir. The chalk ring on the gangway, and McCool standing in it. The signal gun; the rush of feet as the ten hands heaved away on the line. And McCool died, as he had promised, without saying a word.

The body hung at the yard-arm, and as the ship rolled in the swell that came round Berry Head, so the body swung and dangled, doomed to hang there until nightfall, while Hornblower, sick and pale, began to seek out a coaster which planned to call at Dublin from Brixham, so that he could fulfil his half of the bargain. But he could not fulfil it immediately; nor did the dead body hang there for its allotted time. The wind was backing northerly and was showing signs of moderating. A westerly gale would keep the French fleet shut up in Brest; a northerly one might well bring them out, and the Channel Fleet must hurry to its post again. Signals flew from the flagships.

"Hands to the capstan!" bellowed the bosun's mates in twenty-four ships. "Hands make sail!"

With double-reefed topsails set, the ships of the Channel Fleet formed up and began their long slant down-Channel. In the *Renown* it had been, "Mr. Hornblower, see that *that* is disposed of." While the hands laboured at the capstan the corpse was lowered from the yard-arm and sewn into a weighted bit of sailcloth. Clear of Berry Head it was cast overside without ceremony or prayer. McCool had died a felon's death and must be given a felon's burial. And, close-hauled, the big ships clawed their way back to their posts amid the rocks and currents of the Brittany coast. And on board the *Renown* there was one unhappy lieutenant, at least, plagued by dreadful memories.

In the tiny cabin which he shared with Smith there was something that kept Hornblower continually reminded of that morning: the mahogany chest with the name "B. I. McCool" in high relief on the lid. And in Hornblower's letter case lay that last letter and the rambling, delirious poem. Hornblower could send neither on to the widow until the *Renown* should return again to an English harbour, and he was irked that he had not yet fulfilled his half of the bargain. The sight of the chest under his cot jarred on his nerves; its presence in their little cabin irritated Smith.

Hornblower could not rid his memory of McCool;

nor, beating about in a ship of the line on the dreary work of blockade, was there anything to distract him from his obsession. Spring was approaching and the weather was moderating. So that when he opened his leather case and found that letter staring at him again, he felt undiminished that revulsion of spirit. He turned the sheet over; in the half dark of the little cabin he could hardly read the gentle words of farewell. He knew that strange poem almost by heart, and he peered at it again, sacrilege though it seemed to try to analise the thoughts of the brave and frightened man who had written it during his final agony of spirit. "The bee ascends before my rolling eye." What could possibly be the feeling that inspired that strange imagery? "Turn full circle. Turn again." Why should the heavenly powers do that?

A startling thought suddenly began to wake to life in Hornblower's mind. The letter, with its tender phrasing, had been written without correction or erasure. But this poem; Hornblower remembered the discarded sheets covered with scribbling. It had been written with care and attention. A madman, a man distraught with trouble, might produce a meaningless poem with such prolonged effort, but then he would not have written that letter. Perhaps—

Hornblower sat up straight instead of lounging back on his cot. "So strike 'em down." There was no apparent reason why McCool should have written " 'em" instead of "them." Hornblower mouthed the words. To say "them" did not mar either euphony or rhythm. There might be a code. But then why the chest? Why had McCool asked for the chest to be forwarded with its uninteresting contents of clothing? There were two portraits of children; they could easily have been made into a package and sent. The chest with its solid slabs of mahogany and its raised name was a handsome piece of furniture; but it was all very puzzling.

With the letter still in his hand, he got down from the cot and dragged out the chest. B. I. McCool. Barry Ignatius McCool. Payne had gone carefully through the contents of the chest. Hornblower unlocked it and glanced inside again; he could see nothing meriting particular attention, and he closed the lid again and turned the key. B. I. McCool. A secret compartment! In a fever, Hornblower opened the chest again, flung out the contents and examined sides and bottom. It called for only the briefest examination to assure him that there was no room there for anything other than a microscopic secret compartment. The lid was thick and heavy, but he could see nothing suspicious about it. He closed it again and fiddled with the raised letters, without result.

He had actually decided to replace the contents when a fresh thought occurred to him. "The bee ascends!" Feverishly Hornblower took hold of the "B" on the lid. He pushed it, tried to turn it. "The bee ascends!" He put thumb and finger into the two hollows in the loops of the "B," took a firm grip and pulled upward. He was about to give up when the letter yielded a little, rising up out of the lid half an inch. Hornblower opened the box again, and could see nothing different. Fool that he was! "Before my rolling eye." Thumb and forefinger on the "I." First this way, then that way—and it turned!

Still no apparent further result. Hornblower looked at the poem again. "Life still goes on within the heartless town." He could make nothing of that. "Dark forces claim my soul." No. Of course! "Strike 'em down." That " 'em." Hornblower put his hand on the "M" of "McCool" and pressed vigorously. It sank down into the lid. "The sea will rise, the sea will fall." Under firm pressure the first "C" slid upward, the second "C" slid downward. "Turn full circle. Turn again." Round went one "O," and then round went the other in the opposite direction. There was only the "L" now. Hornblower glanced at the poem. "Hell will lift its head." He guessed it at once; he took hold of the top of the "L" and pulled; the letter rose out of the lid as though hinged along the bottom, and at the same moment there was a loud decisive click inside the lid. Nothing else was apparent, and Hornblower gingerly took hold of the lid and lifted it. Only half of it came up; the lower half stayed where it was, and in the oblong hollow between there lay a mass of papers, neatly packaged.

The first package was a surprise. Hornblower, peeping into it, saw that it was a great wad of five-pound notes— a very large sum of money. A second package was similar. Ample money here to finance the opening moves of a new rebellion. The first thing he saw inside the next package was a list of names, with brief explanations written beside each. Hornblower did not have to read very far before he knew that this package contained the information necessary to start the rebellion. In the last package was a draft proclamation ready for printing. "Irishmen!" it began.

Hornblower took his seat on the cot again and tried to think, swaying with the motion of the ship. There was money that would make him rich for life. There was information which, if given to the government, would clutter every gallows in Ireland. Struck by a sudden thought, he put everything back into the chest and closed the lid.

For the moment it was a pleasant distraction, saving him from serious thought, to study the ingenious mechanism of the secret lock. Unless each operation was gone through in turn, nothing happened. The "I" would not turn unless the "B" was first pulled out, and it was most improbable that a casual investigator would pull at that "B" with the necessary force. It was most unlikely that anyone without a clue would ever discover how to open the lid, and the joint in the wood was marvellously well concealed. It occurred to Hornblower that when he should announce his discovery matters would go badly with Payne, who had been charged with searching McCool's effects. Payne would be the laughing-stock of the fleet, a man both damned and condemned.

Hornblower thrust the chest back under the cot and, secure now against any unexpected entrance by Smith, went on to try to think about his discovery. That letter of McCool's had told the truth. "Faithful unto death." McCool's last thought had been for the cause in which he died. If the wind in Tor Bay had stayed westerly another few hours, that chest might have made its way to Dublin. On the other hand, now there would be commendation for him, praise, official notice—all very necessary to a junior lieutenant with no interests behind him to gain him his promotion to captain. And the hangman would have more work to do in Ireland. Hornblower remembered how McCool had died, and felt fresh nausea at the thought. Ireland was quiet now. And the victories of St. Vincent and the Nile and Camperdown had put an end to the imminent danger which England had gone through. England could afford to be merciful. He could afford to be merciful. And the money?

Later on, when Hornblower thought about this incident in his past life, he cynically decided that he resisted temptation because bank notes are tricky things, numbered and easy to trace, and the ones in the chest might even have been forgeries manufactured by the French government. But Hornblower misinterpreted his own motives, possibly in self-defense, because they were so vague and so muddled that he was ashamed of them. He wanted to forget about McCool. He wanted to think of the whole incident as closed.

There were many hours to come of pacing the deck before he reached his decision, and there were several sleepless nights. But Hornblower made up his mind in the end, and made his preparations thoughtfully, and when the time came he acted with decision. It was a quiet evening when he had the first watch; darkness had closed in on the Bay of Biscay, and the *Renown,* under easy sail, was loitering along over the black water with her consorts just in sight. Smith was at cards with the purser and the surgeon in the gunroom. A word from Hornblower sent the two stupidest men of the watch down below to his cabin to carry up the sea-chest, which he had laboriously covered with canvas in preparation for this night. It was heavy, for buried among the clothing inside were two twenty-four-pound shot. They left it in the scuppers at Hornblower's order. And then, when at four bells it was time for the *Renown* to tack, he was able, with one tremendous heave, to throw the thing overboard. The splash went unnoticed as the *Renown* tacked.

There was still that letter. It lay in Hornblower's writing case to trouble him when he saw it. Those tender sentences, that affectionate farewell; it seemed a shame that McCool's widow should not have the privilege of seeing them and treasuring them. But—but— When the *Renown* lay in the Hamoaze, completing for the West Indies, Hornblower found himself sitting at dinner next to Payne. It took a little while to work the conversation around in the right direction.

"By the way," said Hornblower with elaborate casualness, "did McCool leave a widow?"

"A widow? No. Before he left Paris he was involved in a notorious scandal with La Gitanita, the dancer. But no widow."

"Oh," said Hornblower.

That letter, then, was as good a literary exercise as the poem had been. Hornblower realized that the arrival of a

The Last Encounter

ADMIRAL of the Fleet Lord Hornblower sat alone at his dining table at Smallbridge with his glass of port before him; it was a moment of supreme comfort. There was heavy rain beating against the windows; there had been unending rain for days now, a climax to one of the wettest springs in local memory. Every now and again the noise of the rain would increase in volume as gusts of wind drove the heavy drops against the panes. The farmers and the tenants would be complaining worse than ever, now, in the face of the imminent prospect of a harvest ruined before it had begun to ripen, and Hornblower felt distinct satisfaction in the thought that he was not dependent on his rents for his income. As Admiral of the Fleet he could never be on half pay; rain or shine, peace or war, he would receive his very handsome three thousand a year, and with a further three thousand a year from his investments in the Funds he would never again know the pinch of poverty, nor even the need for care. He could be considerate towards his tenants; he might also contrive to allow Richard a further five hundred a year—as Colonel in the Guards with his frequent need for attendance on the young

Queen at court, Richard's tailor's bills must be heavy.

Hornblower took a sip of his port and stretched his legs under the table and enjoyed the warmth of the fire at his back. Two glasses of excellent claret were already playing their part in the digestion of a really superb dinner—that was a further cause for self-congratulation, for at the age of seventy-two he had a digestion that never caused him a moment's disquiet. He was a lucky man: at the head of his profession, at the ultimate, unsurpassable summit (his promotion to Admiral of the Fleet was recent enough to be still a source of unalloyed gratification); in possession of his full health, and enjoying a large income, a loving wife, a fine son, promising grandchildren, and a good cook. He could sip his port and enjoy every drop of it, and when the glass should be empty he would walk through into the drawing room where Barbara would be sitting, reading, and waiting for him beside another roaring fire. He had a wife who loved him, a wife whom the advancing years had strangely made even more beautiful, the sinking of her cheeks calling attention to the magnificent modelling of the bones of her face, her white hair in strange and lovely contrast with her straight back and effortless carriage. She was so beautiful, so gracious, and so dignified. It was the perfect final touch that lately she had had to wear spectacles for reading, which modified her dignity profoundly, so that she always whipped them off when there was a chance of a stranger seeing her. Hornblower could smile again at the thought of it and take another sip of his port; it was better to love a woman than a goddess.

It was strange that he should be so happy and so secure, he who had known so much unhappiness, so much harassing uncertainty, so much peril, and so much hardship. Cannon ball and musket shot, drowning and disease, professional disgrace and military execution; he had escaped by a hair's breadth from them all. He had known the deepest private unhappiness, and now he knew the deepest happiness. He had endured poverty, even hunger, and now he had wealth and security. All very gratifying, said Hornblower to himself; even in his old age he could not address himself without a sneer. "Call no man happy until he is dead," said someone or other, and it was probably true. He was seventy-two, and yet there was still time for this dream that surrounded him to reveal itself as a nightmare.

Characteristically, he had no sooner congratulated himself on his happiness than he began to wonder what would imperil it. Of course; full of good food and before this warm fire he had forgotten the turmoil the world was in. Revolution—anarchy—social upheaval; all Europe, all the world, was in a convulsion of change. Mobs were on the march, and armies too; this year of 1848 would be remembered as a year of destruction—unless its memory should be later overlaid by the memory of years to follow more destructive still. In Paris the barricades were up and a red republic proclaimed. Metternich was in flight from Vienna; the Italian tyrants were in exile from their capitals. In Ireland famine and disease accompanied economic disaster and rebellion. Even here in England the agitators were rousing the mob, and voicing startling demands for parliamentary reform, for better working conditions, for changes which could not amount to less than a social revolution.

Perhaps, old man though he was, he would yet live to see his happiness and security torn from him by an ungrateful fate that made no allowance for his lifelong and kindly liberalism. For six years of his life he had warred against bloody and victory-crazed revolution; for the next fourteen he had warred against the grinding and treacherous tyranny that had inevitably supplanted the revolution. For fourteen years he had staked his life in a struggle against Bonaparte—a struggle with an actual personal aspect, growing more and more personal as he gained promotion. He had fought for liberty, for freedom, but that did not make the fight a less personal one. In two hemispheres, on fifty coasts, Hornblower had fought for liberty and Bonaparte for tyranny, and the struggle had ended in Bonaparte's fall. For nearly thirty years Bonaparte had been in his grave, and Hornblower was now sitting with a comfortable fire warming his back and a glass of excellent port warming his interior; but at the same time, in typical fashion, he was impairing his happiness by wondering whether it might be taken from him.

The wind shook the house again and the rain roared against the windowpanes. The dining room door opened silently and Brown, the butler, came in to put more coal on the fire. Like the good servant he was, he searched the room with his eyes to see that all was well; his unobtrusive glance took note of the fact that Hornblower had not yet finished his first glass of port; the knowledge would be helpful in timing exactly the bringing of the coffee into the drawing room when Hornblower should decide to move.

Faintly through the house came the jangle of the front door bell; now who could possibly be ringing at the door at eight o'clock at night, on a night like this? It could not be a tenant—tenants would go to the side door if by any chance they had business at the house—and no caller was expected. Hornblower felt the urgings of curiosity, especially as the bell jangled a second time almost before its first janglings had died away. The dining room windows and doors shook a trifle, indicating that the footman had opened the front door. Hornblower pricked up his ears; he imagined that he could hear voices in the outer hall.

"Go and see who that is, Brown," he ordered.

"Yes, my lord."

There had been many years when "Aye aye, sir," had been Brown's reply to an order, but Brown never forgot that he was now a butler, and butler to a peer at that. He walked silently across the room—and Hornblower, even while wondering who the caller might be, found himself as usual admiring the cut of Brown's evening clothes. The perfection of cut, and yet with just that something about it to make it plain to the discriminating observer that they were a butler's clothes and not a gentleman's.

Brown silently shut the door behind him, and Hornblower wished he had not, for in the interval while the door was open and Brown was passing through, there had been a tantalising moment when conversation could be heard—a loud, rather harsh voice making some sort of demand and the footman responding with unyielding deference.

Even now when the door was shut, Hornblower believed he could hear that harsh voice, and curiosity completely overcame him. He rose and pulled at the bell cord beside the fire. Brown came in again, and with the opening of the door the harsh voice became distinctly audible.

"What the devil's going on, Brown?" demanded Hornblower.

"I'm afraid it's a lunatic, my lord."

"A lunatic?"

"He says he's Napoleon Bonaparte, my lord."

"God bless my soul! And what does he want here?"

Even at seventy-two there was a little tingle of quickened blood in arteries and veins at the chance of action. A man who thought he was the long-dead emperor might well intend causing trouble when coming to the house of Admiral of the Fleet Lord Hornblower. But Brown's next words were not so promising of trouble.

"He wishes to borrow a carriage and horses, my lord."

"What for?"

"It seems there has been trouble on the railway, my

lord. He says he must reach Dover as soon as possible to catch the Calais packet. His business, he says, is of the greatest importance."

"What is he like?"

"He is dressed like a gentleman, my lord."

"H'm."

It was not so very long ago that the railway had made its way round the edge of the park at Smallbridge, sullying the fair fields of Kent on its way to Dover. From the upper windows of the house the foul smoke of the engines could be seen, and the raucous sound of their whistles could be heard. But the worst prognostications of the pessimists had not been realised. The cows still gave down their milk, the pigs still farrowed, the orchards still bore their fruit, and there had been singularly few accidents.

"Will that be all, my lord?" asked Brown, recalling his master to the fact that there was still an intruder in the outer hall who had to be dealt with.

"No. Bring him in here," said Hornblower. The life of a country gentleman might be pleasant and secure, but sometimes it was damnably dull.

"Very good, my lord."

Hornblower took a glance in the ormolu mirror over the fireplace as Brown withdrew; his cravat and his shirt front were in good order, the sparse white hairs were tidy, and there was something of the old twinkle in the brown eyes under the snow-white eyebrows. Brown returned and held the door as he made his announcement.

"Mr. Napoleon Bonaparte."

It was not the figure that pictures had made so familiar that came into the room. No green coat and white breeches, no cocked hat and epaulettes; the man who entered wore a civilian suit of grey, visible under an unbuttoned cloak. The grey suit was nearly black with wet; the man was soaked to the skin, and as high as the knees of his tight strapped trousers he was plastered with mud; but he would have been a dandy had his clothes not been in so deplorable a condition. There was something about his figure that might remind one of the dead Bonaparte—the short legs that made his height a little below average—and there might be something about the grey eyes that studied Hornblower so keenly in the candlelight, but the rest of his appearance was unexpected—not even a parody or a travesty of the emperor. He actually wore a heavy moustache and a little tuft of beard—as if anyone could imagine the great Napoleon with a moustache!—and instead of the short hair with the lock drooping on the forehead this man wore his hair fashionably long; it would have been in ringlets over the ears if it had not been so wet that it hung in rat's-tails.

"Good evening, sir," said Hornblower.

"Good evening. Lord Hornblower, I understand?"

"That is so."

The newcomer spoke good English, with a decided accent. But it did not seem to be the accent of a Frenchman.

"I must apologise for intruding upon you at this time."

Mr. Bonaparte's gesture towards the polished dining

table showed that he was appreciative of the importance of the period of digestion after dinner.

"Please do not give it another thought, sir," said Hornblower. "And if it should be more convenient for you to speak French, pray do so."

"French or English is equally convenient to me, my lord. Or German or Italian, for that matter."

Again that was not like the emperor—his Italian had been bad and he spoke no English at all. A strange sort of madman this must be. The stranger's cloak had opened a little further, and Hornblower could see a broad red ribbon and the glitter of a star. The man was wearing the Grand Eagle of the Legion of Honour, Napoleon's own rank; indeed he must be insane. One final test—

"How should I address you, sir?" asked Hornblower.

"As Your Highness, if you could be so good, my lord. Or as Monseigneur—that might be more convenient."

"Very well, Your Highness. My butler gave me a not very clear account of how I might be of service to Your Highness. Perhaps your Highness would be kind enough to command me?"

"The kindness is yours, my lord. I tried to explain to your butler that the railway line beside your park has been blocked. The train I was in was unable to proceed farther."

"Most regrettable, Your Highness. These modern inventions . . ."

"They have their inconveniences. I understand that as a result of the recent heavy rain the embankment in what they call a cutting has given way, and a large mass of earth, to the amount of some hundreds of tons, has fallen on the rails."

"Indeed, Your Highness?"

"Yes. I was given to understand that it might even be a matter of some days before the line is clear again. And my business is of an importance which will not brook the delay of a single hour."

"Naturally, Your Highness. Affairs of state are invariably pressing."

This madman talked a strange mixture of sanity and nonsense; and he reacted to Hornblower's heavy-handed humour quite convincingly. The heavy eyelids raised themselves a trifle, and the cold grey eyes searched Hornblower's.

"You speak truth, my lord, without, I fear, giving it its full weight. My business is of the greatest importance. Not only does the fate of France hinge upon my arrival in Paris, but the future history of the world—the whole destiny of mankind!"

"The name of Bonaparte implies nothing less, Your Highness," said Hornblower.

"Europe is falling into anarchy. She is a prey to traitors, self-seekers, idealogues, demagogues, of uncounted fools and of knaves without number. France under strong guidance again can give order back to the world."

"Your Highness says no more than the truth."

"Then you will appreciate the urgency of my business,

my lord. The elections are about to be held in Paris, and I must be there—I must be there within forty-eight hours. That is the reason why I waded through mud under a deluge of rain to your house."

The stranger looked down at his mud-daubed clothes and at the trickles of water draining from them.

"I could find Your Highness a change of clothing," suggested Hornblower.

"No time for that, even, thank you, my lord. Farther down the railway line, beyond this unfortunate landslide, and beyond the tunnel—I think at a place called Maidstone—I can board another train which will take me to Dover. From thence the steam packet to Calais—the train to Paris—and my destiny!"

"So Your Highness wishes to be driven to Maidstone?"

"Yes, my lord."

It was eight miles of fairly easy road; not an impossibly extravagant request from a stranger in distress. But the wind was southwesterly—Hornblower pulled himself up with a jerk. These steam packets paid no attention to wind or tide, although it was hard for a man who had all his life commanded sailing vessels to remember it. The madman had a sane enough plan up to a point—as far as Paris. There he would presumably be put away in an asylum where he would be harmless and unharmed. Not even the excitable French would do anything to injure so entertaining an eccentric.

But—Hornblower changed his mind again. It would

be hard on the coachman to have to turn out on a night like this and drive sixteen miles at a madman's whim. He was wondering how to decline the request without hurting the poor soul's feelings when the door from the drawing room opened to admit Barbara. She was tall and straight and beautiful and dignified; now that the years had made Hornblower stoop-shouldered her eyes were on a level with his.

"Horatio—" she began, and then paused when she saw the stranger; but someone who knew Barbara well—Hornblower, for instance—might guess that perhaps she had not been unaware of the presence of a stranger in the dining room before she entered, and that perhaps she had come in like this to find out what was going on. Undoubtedly she had removed her spectacles for this public appearance.

The stranger came to polite attention in the presence of a lady.

"May I have the honour of presenting my wife to Your Highness?" asked Hornblower.

The stranger made a low bow, and, advancing, took Barbara's hand and bent low again to kiss it. Hornblower watched with some little annoyance. Barbara was woman enough to be susceptible to a kiss on the hand—any rascal could find his way into her good graces if he could perform that outlandish ceremony in the right way.

"The beautiful Lady Hornblower," said the stranger. "Wife of the most distinguished sailor in Her Majesty's

Navy, sister of the great Duke—but best known as the beautiful Lady Hornblower."

This madman had a way with him, as well as being well informed. But the speech was thoroughly out of character, of course; Napoleon had always been notorious for his brusquerie with women, and had been said to limit his conversation with them to questions about the number of their children. But it would never occur to Barbara to think like that when such a speech had just been made to her. She turned inquiring blue eyes on her husband.

"His Highness . . ." began Hornblower.

He played the farce out to the end, recounting the stranger's request and laying stress on the importance of his arrival in Paris.

"You have already ordered the carriage, I suppose, Horatio?" asked Barbara.

"As a matter of fact I haven't, yet."

"Then of course you will. Every minute is of importance, as His Highness says."

"You are too kind, my dear lady," said His Highness.

"But—" began Hornblower, and under her gaze he said no more. He walked across and pulled at the bell cord, and when Brown appeared he gave the necessary instructions.

"Tell Harris he can have five minutes to put the horses to. Not a second longer," supplemented Barbara.

"Yes, my lady."

"My lady, my lord," said the stranger as Brown withdrew. "All Europe will be in your debt for this act of kindness. The world is notoriously ungrateful, but I hope the gratitude of Bonaparte will be unmistakable."

"Your Highness is too kind," said Hornblower, trying not to be too sarcastic.

"I hope Your Highness has a pleasant journey," said Barbara, "and a successful one."

The fellow had won every bit of Barbara's esteem, obviously. She ignored her husband's indignant glances until Brown announced the carriage and the stranger had rolled away into the deluging rain.

"But my dear—" protested Hornblower at last. "What on earth did you do that for?"

"It'll do Harris no harm to drive to Maidstone and back," said Barbara. "The horses are never exercised enough in any case."

"But the man was mad," said Hornblower. "A raving lunatic. A stark, staring, idiotic imposter, and not a very good impostor at that."

"I think there was something about him," said Barbara, sticking to her guns. "Something . . ."

"You mean he kissed your hand and made pretty speeches," said Hornblower in a huff.

It was not until six days later that *The Times* published a dispatch from Paris.

Prince Louis Napoleon Bonaparte, the Pretender to the Imperial Throne, had been nominated as a candidate in the elections about to be held for the Presidency of the French Republic.

And it was not until a month after that that a liveried

servant delivered a packet and a letter at Smallbridge. The letter was in French, but Hornblower had no difficulty in translating it.

MY LORD:

I am commanded by Monseigneur His Highness the Prince-President, as one of his first acts on assuming the control of the affairs of his people, to convey to you His Highness's gratitude for the assistance you were kind enough to render him during his journey to Paris. Accompanying this letter Your Lordship will find the insignia of a Chevalier of the Legion of Honour, and I have the pleasure of assuring Your Lordship that at His Highness's command I am requesting of Her Majesty the Queen, through Her Majesty's Secretary of State for Foreign Affairs, permission for you to accept them.

I am also commanded by His Highness to beg that you will convey to Her Ladyship your wife his grateful thanks, and that you will present for her acceptance the accompanying token of his esteem and regard, which His Highness hopes will be a fitting tribute to the beautiful eyes which His Highness remembers so well.

With the highest expressions of my personal regard, I am,

Your most humble and obedient servant,
CADORE, *Minister of Foreign Affairs*

"Humbug!" said Hornblower. "The fellow will be calling himself emperor before you can say Jack Robinson. Napoleon the Third, I suppose."

"I said there was something about him," said Barbara. "This is a very beautiful sapphire."

It certainly matched the eyes into which Hornblower smiled with tender resignation.